Secrets...
& Freedom

...*Plus!*

COULD **YOU** MAKE THE FIRST MOVE?
TRY OUR FAB QUIZ AT
THE BACK OF THE BOOK

SOME SECRETS ARE JUST TOO GOOD TO KEEP TO YOURSELF!

Sugar
SECRETS...

...& Freedom

Mel Sparke

Collins
An Imprint of HarperCollinsPublishers

Published in Great Britain by Collins in 1999
Collins is an imprint of HarperCollins*Publishers* Ltd
77–85 Fulham Palace Road, Hammersmith, London W6 8JB

The HarperCollins website address is
www.**fire**and**water**.com

9 8 7 6 5 4 3 2 1

Creative consultant: Karen McCombie
Copyright © Sugar 1999. Licensed withTLC.

ISBN 0 00 675442 2

Printed and bound in Great Britain by
Caledonian International Book Manufacturing Ltd, Glasgow

CHAPTER 1

· ·

PARENTS: WHO'D HAVE 'EM?

Scooping up her long dark hair in her hands, Maya Joshi twisted it into a loose knot and fastened it with a butterfly clip while gazing out of the open kitchen window. Oblivious to everything around her, including the family meal she was currently a part of, Maya idly watched the golden evening sun dapple the pale green leaves of the mock orange bush with soft light.

Closing her eyes, she breathed in the heavy scent of the honeysuckle that curled its way around the arch at the side of the house. Maya loved summer. Lazy days like she'd had today, hanging out in the park with Sonja, Kerry and the others, catching some sun, fooling around, having a laugh. Summer: long days, warm nights, no homework, no school, no pressure – just freedom...

Eyes still closed, Maya suddenly felt the softest, lightest stroke across her ankle. Half tickly, half delicious, she knew at once who was responsible for the sensation. Marcus. He must have sneaked in from the garden without anyone noticing – her parents certainly wouldn't approve if they knew he was around.

Turning and looking down at her plate, Maya deftly scooped some butter off her bread with her little finger and held it under the table. A strangely rough tongue licked it off while the Burmese curled his tail gratefully around her calf.

Unfortunately, Marcus was in the mood for more.

"Aaaaark!" he croaked loudly.

"Maya! How many times have we told you we don't want the cat in the kitchen while we're eating?" said her mother, looking across the table at her sternly. "And please don't play with your hair at the table either!"

"But I'm not– I mean, I didn't let Marcus in!" Maya protested. She hated being accused of something she hadn't done. "He must have—"

"Maya, listen to your mother, please, and get that cat out of here!" her father interrupted, in his that's-the-end-of-that-conversation voice. It was the same voice that managed to reduce adult patients to nervous little kids in Dr Sanjay Joshi's surgery.

On the other side of the table, Maya's little brother Ravi bobbed down to look at the unwelcome guest. Sunny was wearing her best as-good-as-gold expression as she smugly watched her big sister stand up and shoo the reluctant Marcus out of the room.

Maya gently pushed him by the bottom through the gap in the door, but Marcus did his special trick of turning into an origami cat, flipping around magically to face her. Staring up at his favourite member of the family, he bawled his indignation.

"Aaaaark! Eeee-aaark!"

Maya couldn't help grinning – Marcus had the most un-pussy cat voice. No pretty purring and delicate miaows for him. "It's like listening to a nail being dragged down a blackboard!" Sonja Harvey had once said, and it was the best description Maya had heard of Marcus's screechings.

"Come on, now. Hurry up!" her dad's voice came impatiently from behind and Maya dropped her smile. Pushing Marcus more firmly out of the kitchen and into the hall, she closed the door behind him and returned to her place at the table.

"So, what's on everyone's schedule this week?" her mother asked brightly, gazing round the table at her three children.

Here we go, sighed Maya to herself. *The Sunday night interrogation. Even though it's the holidays, we still have to go through this.*

In term time, the Sunday evening meal was the point in the week where the three younger members of the Joshi family discussed with their parents what lessons, essays, projects or tests lay ahead in the coming days. Sanjay and Nina Joshi were big believers in discussion – but only, it seemed to Maya, when it came to homework. Or revision. Or getting those top-grade marks.

And apart from keeping their parents up to speed on school work, it was also the time when the three children could bring up any plans they had – for parental discussion and approval. Or disapproval, as the case may be.

"I've got an extra rehearsal for the summer school play on Saturday. You haven't forgotten, have you, Mummy?" said Sunny, so sweetly it almost made Maya's teeth hurt. Both parents smiled indulgently at their thirteen-year-old daughter.

"No, of course not," said Nina Joshi. "But what about your art project, Sunita? You're not letting this play get in the way of that, are you?"

"No, of course not, Mummy – I've nearly finished it!" Sunny chirped.

And you wouldn't have got on so far if I hadn't

helped you out with it, with no thanks, thought Maya darkly. *But you might as well make the most of it, Sunny. Once it comes to choosing your subjects at school next year, Mum and Dad aren't going to let you carry on with the fun stuff like drama and art.*

"Mum, it's Calum's birthday party next Saturday afternoon!" Ravi piped up, his big brown eyes wide with excitement.

"Well, so it is," smiled his mother. "Your sister can take you shopping for a present this week and she can drop you off there on Saturday. All right, Maya?"

It wasn't all right with Maya, but there was no point in arguing. Her parents' attitude was that the whole family should look after one another. But, being the eldest, Maya seemed to do a whole lot of looking after with nothing much in return. Unless you counted being continually pushed to study – at the expense of a social life or anything else that was remotely fun. And that certainly seemed to be her parents' way of showing they cared.

"Maya?" her father looked over at her sharply. "Did you hear what your mother said?"

"Yes, of course – it's fine," she nodded, giving her adorable little brother a smile. He grinned back, showing off his two new chunky front teeth.

It always surprised Maya to see little signs that he was growing up – for her, seven-year-old Ravi would forever be her cuddly baby bro. It was a far cry from how she saw Sunny, who'd always seemed much smarter than her years and who knew exactly how to get her own way, whatever the circumstances.

The reason Maya had wanted to keep Saturday afternoon free was pathetic really; she wanted to go shopping for pyjamas. Sonja was having a sleepover on Saturday – not the normal girls' night in, but a proper, giggly, silly sleepover.

For Sonja, Kerry and Cat, it was a nostalgic thing to do – they'd had loads of sleepovers together in the past. But for Maya, it was all new. Not just because she had only known the others for eighteen months or so, but because staying the night at friends' houses was something her parents had frowned on when she was younger. Now she was sixteen, they could hardly complain, but Maya was still faced with the problem of what to wear.

Was her long cotton nightie too mumsy-looking? Would the others have cool and cute PJs, or was that out too? Perhaps she should just take a pair of leggings and an old T-shirt to sleep in.

Maya knew that Cat and Sonja would laugh if they found out that she was worried about something so trivial, which was why she'd asked Kerry to go shopping with her on Saturday afternoon. They couldn't go before then because Kerry had a holiday job at a chemist's during the week.

But Maya could rely on Kerry not to tease her, and to understand her self-consciousness. If there was one thing Maya hated more than anything it was feeling like the odd one out. But she often did, more than anyone knew – even her best friends.

What to wear for a sleepover wasn't the only thing bothering her. When Maya had been in the End-of-the-Line café the day before with Matt and Joe, Ollie had told them about an indie night at The Bell on Friday. Everyone in their crowd was right up for it and all set to go. But then, not everyone had Maya's parents...

This is ridiculous, thought Maya, squirming in her chair. *I'm sixteen years old, I'm worrying about what pyjamas to wear and I'm scared to ask my parents if I can go out with my friends...*

"Sonja and everyone are going to a club on Friday night and I'd like to go too," she found herself blurting out, before she could worry about it further.

"A club? Where exactly?" asked her father, his fork paused in mid-air.

"At The Bell," she answered, hoping they wouldn't realise exactly where she meant.

"The Bell..." her father ruminated. "What, you mean that pub off the High Street?"

"It's– it's more of a venue than a pub," Maya waffled, knowing that her chances of going had dropped from poor to zero.

"Oh, no, young lady. You know full well that you're under age for that sort of thing and you know it's not the kind of place I would expect my daughter to be seen in!"

"But you know I don't drink!" Maya appealed to her father. "I only want to go because of the music and to be with my friends—"

"Now come on, Maya," said her mother in an attempt to pacify her. "Apart from anything else, you're already going out on Saturday evening."

As ever, when it came to her parents, Maya swallowed her objections. She stared down at her plate, anger burning inside her. How could her mother class sitting around in Sonja's bedroom as 'going out'? And why couldn't they both just trust her for once when she said she didn't touch alcohol?

On top of the indignity of it all, she could sense the smirk on Sunny's face, even though she couldn't see it.

"So what will you be doing in maths club this

week, Maya?" her mother asked, changing the subject to one that didn't exactly lift her eldest daughter's spirits.

"I've no idea," said Maya blankly.

Summer holidays equal freedom? Who am I kidding? she thought hopelessly.

Her parents had enrolled Sunny into a full-time summer school and Maya into a day-a-week maths club, complete with homework. Ravi had got off lightly, which caused problems for Maya: his part-time holiday club meant plenty of part-time babysitting for her.

Maya felt resentment bubble in her chest. The rules and regulations she could cope with. The stupid maths club and the unpaid nannying she could just about handle. But the constant refusal to recognise that she was sixteen, that she needed to have her own life...

I feel like I'm suffocating!

Maya stared fixedly at her plate as she willed the hot tears not to spill out of her eyes.

Something– something's got to change! And soon...

Apart from the clanking of forks and knives on plates, only one sound broke the awkward silence hanging over the dinner table.

"Aaaark!" came a muffled cry from outside the kitchen door.

• • •

Ten minutes' walk away, in a house across from the park, Joe Gladwin shovelled peas from one side of his plate to the other. He was not in the mood for eating, nor was he in the mood for listening to what his mother had to say.

"Joe, darling? What do you think?"

"I think I don't want to do it," he answered through gritted teeth.

"But, Joe, you haven't been to see him for ever such a long time..."

"Look, I'm sixteen, Mum. Going to spend the weekend with my dad and his girlfriend isn't exactly thrilling. You know what I mean?"

"Yes, but Joe – he is your dad..." Automatically, Susie Gladwin reached across and pushed her son's tangled brown hair away from his face.

"Mum!" Joe flicked her hand away in irritation.

She looked at him apologetically. "Sorry, darling."

Joe's nostrils flared, but he tried to keep his temper. After all, it wasn't really the hair-stroking or the 'darling' stuff that was getting on his nerves (although both of these, along with all his mother's other over-protective habits, did drive him mad). It was more the whole idea of being 'summoned' to see a father he couldn't stand – *and* the fact that his mum seemed to want him to go.

He took a calming breath before he spoke.

"Mum, why are you so keen for me to visit him? It's not like he's your favourite person either."

"I know, darling," nodded his mother, reaching out to pat her son's hand. "It's just that it has been a long time since you saw him and I don't want him thinking that I'm, well, *keeping* you from going."

"Oh, for God's sake, Mum! It's not like I'm some three-year-old and you're trying to snatch me away! I think I'm old enough to decide when I do and don't want to see my own father!"

"Yes, I know, sweetheart, but your dad might not see it that way..."

Joe noticed with alarm that his mum looked uncomfortably close to crying.

Oh no, not that, he sighed to himself.

"OK, OK," he said, holding up his hands in defeat. "I'll do it."

Although after what Dad did to Mum, I know what I'd really like to do, thought Joe bitterly. *Never have to see my scumbag of a father again...*

CHAPTER 2

• •

HOME TRUTHS

"Sounds like your Sunday night was as bad as mine," sighed Maya as she sat with the rest of the crowd in the End-of-the-Line café.

"Yeah?" said Joe. "What's happened with you?"

Joe was keen to hear someone else's moans – it made him feel better about his own predicament. He'd just told his friends about the previous evening, which had gone even further downhill after he'd agreed to the parental visit.

His mum had made him call up his father there and then, which was bad enough. But after a few awkward words and arrangements, his dad had had the not-so-brilliant notion to pass him on to Gillian. Trying to make polite conversation with the woman your dad had run off with wasn't exactly the easiest thing in the world.

A sudden thump on his arm brought Joe down to earth again.

"What are you talking about now? You're not still moaning on about your dad are you, Joe?" said Ollie Stanton playfully, pulling up a seat from another table and joining his friends at the booth in the big bay window of the café.

He knew how difficult Joe found the situation with his dad and, while he was glad Joe was opening up about it in front of the others, he also instinctively felt that a bit of humour would lighten things up.

"And what are *you* doing, Ollie?" Sonja teased him. "Skiving off on another break?"

"Well, there's hardly anyone in except you lot," he grinned, gazing round the café. "And I'm sure my fellow workers can spare me for a moment."

"Oi!" called Anna from behind the counter, flinging a balled-up tea towel at his head.

Stretching out, Matt caught the unravelling cloth neatly, before it could land smack-bang on Catrina Osgood's perfectly made-up face.

"Sorry, Catrina!" Anna apologised. "I was aiming for the lazy little git in the apron, but he ducked."

"Don't worry about it, Anna – I'll kick him for

you, if you like," Cat replied brightly. "If that's OK with you, Kerry?"

Kerry shrugged. "Oh, go ahead. He's a rotten boyfriend anyway."

"Why am I a rotten boyfriend?" Ollie blinked pitifully at Kerry.

"'Cause you got us all excited about that indie night at The Bell on Friday and you went and got the date wrong!" she said, trying to sound stern – but spoiling it all by breaking into a grin.

"*What?*" yelped Sonja and Matt in unison.

"OK, I'm guilty – it's on *next* month. Oops!" shrugged Ollie.

"You mean I went through a whole heap of hassle with my parents for nothing last night?"

Everyone turned to look at Maya. For the first time, they noticed that her normally serene expression had vanished. Instead, she seemed tense and brushed her curtains of shiny dark hair back behind her ears in a more agitated way than usual.

"So, uh, what's the story? What went on last night?" asked Joe, realising that he'd already asked this question, but never received a reply.

"Oh, just the usual rubbish," Maya snapped unhappily. "Just *no*, you can't do this; *no*, you can't do that; *no*, you can't be trusted. That sort of thing."

The others were silent for a second: the one person they never expected to lose her cool was Maya, and here she was on the verge of... something.

"But what's all this about, Maya?" asked Cat, studying her friend's face. She was aware that she never completely understood Maya – after all, Cat spent most of her time thinking about herself – but to see her friend looking so upset was unnerving. "I mean, we know your folks are hot on you studying all the time and everything, but you get on pretty well with them, don't you?"

"Oh, *yes*," answered Maya, laying on the sarcasm thick. "I get on great with them as long as I *get* good grades, *look* after my brother and sister, *do* what I'm told – and have *no life!*"

Once again, everyone was stumped. Maya never flipped out. Maya never had problems. She was the one who sailed sensibly through everything; she was the one who was reasoned, calm and balanced, while Cat, Sonja, Joe, Kerry, Matt or Ollie goofed up, stressed out or said the wrong thing.

Maya was untouchable, unshakeable – she was the rock among them. Now something *had* shaken her up, and that rattled them all.

"But I thought you kind of got off on all that studying?" said Sonja lamely.

Maya rolled her eyes. "Just because I'm smart doesn't mean I *enjoy* everything I do."

Coming from anyone else it might have sounded big-headed, but they all understood what Maya meant. The top stream in every subject was her natural home and no one could deny how brainy she was.

"OK, so your parents are a bit strict and everything," Sonja continued, trying to make sense of what was going on, "but they don't stop you coming out with us, do they?"

As soon as the words were out of her mouth, everyone realised that that wasn't quite true. There had been plenty of occasions when Maya had bailed out from an outing and none of them had ever pushed her for an explanation. Without spelling it out, they understood that when Maya said no, she meant no, and it wasn't necessarily her choice.

"But even during term time, you're here most days after school with us, aren't you?" Kerry ventured, trying to say something positive.

Maya gave a hollow laugh. "Yes, but only because my parents assume I'm actually at home studying. By the time Mum commutes back from the city and Dad finishes surgery, it's nearly seven. I'm always safely back in my room by then, working hard like the good little daughter I'm supposed to be."

"What about the nights we all go out?" asked Joe, amazed at the notion of Maya being in any way a liar. "What do you tell them then?"

"Oh, I try to stick to the truth – it's just that I usually don't tell them the *whole* truth," she answered, her gaze dropping to the table. "It's like, when I've been to see bands with you guys... well, I tell them it's a concert. And that seems fine, as long as they don't realise it's in the back of a pub or in a venue that has a bar or whatever."

"What about my parties? You come to plenty of them," said Matt.

His house parties were legendary: a den with its own sound system, a fridge full of pizza and beer – Matt was never short of guests.

"Well, they've never met your dad, but they know who he is," Maya pointed out, referring to Matt's very influential, very rich, property developer father. "That makes you sound quite respectable."

Cat burst out laughing. "Mr Love Pants!? Respectable? Who are you kidding?"

Matt shot her a cutting look. The last thing needed at this point was any of Cat's barbed comments.

"Of course, the other thing is..." Maya hesitated. "Well, they think you're only sixteen."

"What?" Matt burst out, suddenly offended.

"And they think you're still at Bartdale's."

"But I left the place more than a year ago!" protested Matt, shuddering at the memory of the private school where he'd boarded for more years than he cared to remember.

"Yes, but if I told them you were an eighteen-year-old unemployed wannabe DJ, who dossed around at his daddy's expense, hosting wild parties whenever possible, do you think they'd let me set foot in your driveway, never mind your house?"

"Uh, I guess not," said Matt, reeling slightly from Maya's unflattering description.

"Ouch!" said Ollie quietly, wincing as he watched Matt wither under Maya's gaze.

Matt prided himself on being up with the latest dance music, up with the latest fashion, popular with half the girls in Winstead – wait a minute, make that the *county*. To find himself reduced by Maya to the level of chancer/scrounger took his breath away.

But then that was Maya for you. Kerry was just a sweetheart, Sonja was his buddy and Cat – well, Cat was another matter. But Maya could always slay him with her ultra-direct way of talking.

"It's just that I've had enough of it," Maya pronounced, closing her eyes and rubbing her forehead with the palm of her hand. A vision of

22

her father reading over her homework before she handed it in appeared annoyingly in her head. Wasn't that what teachers were there for?

"So what are you going to do?" asked Kerry, peering earnestly through her wire-rimmed specs.

"That's the problem," sighed Maya despairingly, without opening her eyes. "What the hell *can* I do?"

CHAPTER 3

• •

SNAP DECISION

"Eurghhh – I don't like them!" said Ravi, pointing
at the courgettes that Brigid was cutting up for the
vegetable lasagne.

"Well, everybody else does, so you know what
you can do, don't you?" said Brigid, busily making
dinner for the Joshi family.

"What?" said Ravi, looking up at Brigid's
serious face.

"Pick them out!" she grinned, putting down
her knife and tickling him.

Pulling her books out from her bag, Maya
smiled as she watched Ravi and Brigid muck
around.

Brigid was wonderful – she'd helped the family
out since they moved to Winstead from the city,
her official duties being to pick Ravi up from

school (or holiday club now that it was summer), oversee homework (which still went on in the Joshi household, even if didn't in any other family's at this time of year) and make dinner in time for Maya's parents coming home.

But apart from that, the jolly, fifty-something Irish woman was a good friend to all the Joshi children – happy to sit and play Jenga with Ravi, to listen to Sunny witter on about her favourite boy bands and, most of all, to keep schtum about Maya's after-school activities.

"Ravi – would you look at you!" Brigid suddenly gasped. "I take it you did some painting at your group today?"

"Uh-huh?" he nodded up at her.

"Well, did you not know you're meant to put paint on to paper, not your hands!"

Ravi looked down at his paint-splattered hands.

"Go on and get them washed!" Brigid chided him gently and watched him trotting off. Then, halting her chopping for a second, she looked over her shoulder at Maya. "And what would be the matter with you? You're not looking too happy. Is it the Monday blues?"

"Oh, I'm a bit fed up generally, that's all," Maya answered. It was an understatement, but she didn't want to moan on to Brigid; she'd just spent an hour doing that to her friends down at the End. And although it had been a relief to talk about it, it hadn't actually solved anything or helped her feel any better.

"You know what you need, don't you?" said Brigid.

A different life? thought Maya, but instead said, "What's that, then, Brigid?"

"A hobby," said Brigid firmly. "What with all your studying, even in the holidays, you could really do with something else to get the brain cells going in a different way."

"What, like knitting?" Maya laughed.

"No, y'daft thing!" Brigid laughed back. "Now, for example, my niece Ashleigh – she's just started going to a photography club at the Downfield Adult Education Centre. D'you know it?"

"Yes, my friends Joe and Ollie live near there," nodded Maya, suddenly remembering a photography project she'd done in Year Eight as part of her art class. Four of them had worked on it, recording a day in the life of the animal shelter in the city – it had been brilliant fun. "But it'll just be for adults then..."

"Oh no, this class is especially for teenagers. My Ashleigh's been going for a couple of weeks now. She saw a poster for it on the notice board when she was passing."

Brigid went back to chopping the courgettes, leaving Maya deep in thought.

• • •

Maya was still thinking about it later that evening, when she glanced into the living room and saw that her parents were absorbed in the nine o'clock news.

"I'm just going to make a quick phone call," she said from the doorway, trying to sound casual. Her father turned round and nodded at her.

"Close the door then, so we can hear the television."

"Sure," she replied, grabbing the handle. It wasn't as though Maya wanted them to hear her conversation anyway.

Pulling the phone lead as far from the living room as it would go, Maya sat herself on the bottom of the stairs and dialled.

"Hello?"

"Hi, Mrs Gladwin? It's Maya. Is Joe there?"

"Certainly, dear! Hold on!"

In the muffled distance, Maya could hear Joe saying, "What, Maya – for *me*?" It was typical Joe: he was only just getting more confident at speaking to his girl mates face to face, but for some reason, over the phone, he still reverted to being Shy Boy extraordinaire.

"Maya?" he said tentatively, picking up the receiver at last.

"Hi, Joe! Did you stay down at the End for much longer after I left tonight?"

"Er, nah."

"Well, listen – I need a favour..."

"Er, OK."

I wish he wouldn't get like this, thought Maya, aware of how tongue-tied he was. *I know he's nervous with girls as a whole, but you'd think he'd be used to us lot by now...*

"You know the Downfield Adult Education Centre?" she continued.

"Sure."

"Listen – on their notice board there's some information about a photography club. Can you check it out for me and let me know what it says?"

"Sure."

"Brilliant! Thanks! Well, I've got my maths thing tomorrow, but I'll see you down the End after that, OK?"

"Sure."

"Bye, Joe."

"Er, yeah, bye!"

Oh, Joe, you are a funny guy, smiled Maya, putting down the phone. Immediately, her mind turned to her old school project. Where were those photos packed away? She'd love to dig them out and look at them again...

Lost in thought, Maya didn't register the creak of the bedroom door at the top of the stairs, let alone notice Sunny disappearing into her room after earwigging her big sister's conversation.

• • •

Joe kicked a stone off the pavement and wondered what to say next.

It was Wednesday afternoon and, having nothing better to do, Joe had called in for Maya before going to the café. But now he wished he hadn't. Strolling along the road together, the silence was almost painful. He shot a sidelong glance at Maya and saw her gazing at her watch for what felt like the fiftieth time in the last five minutes.

"Yes, it's *still* 4.30 and it's *still* only Wednesday!" he felt like teasing her, but, being Joe, he gulped down the words and shrugged instead.

Joe hated this feeling of struggling to communicate with his mates – the female ones especially.

Like on the phone, the other night... He winced

at the memory. *How much of a gimp must I have sounded to Maya?*

It was fine when Maya and Sonja and the others did most of the talking; he could relax then and start to join in without being too swamped with awkwardness. But when there were silences like this... he felt that if he dared open his mouth, stupid words would tumble out and hang in the air in a big speech bubble.

You're mad, you know that? he told himself. *She's unhappy, she's your friend – just talk to her!*

"Hey, smile! It may never, er, happen..." he said limply, imagining that speech bubble bobbing above his head.

"Sorry, Joe, I was miles away," Maya answered, trying to force the corners of her mouth into a positive shape.

"Penny for 'em?"

Oh God, Joe! he cringed inwardly. *You're sounding like your mother...*

"What?" asked Maya, momentarily confused.

"Er, your thoughts. Penny for your thoughts." Joe felt his cheeks flush as he spelt out his lame comment. Actually, for a second there, looking all wrapped up in her thoughts, Maya had reminded him slightly of Kerry. Which made him blush even more.

"Right, right," said Maya vaguely. "It's just,

well, you know that photography club you found out about for me?"

"Yeah, sure," Joe nodded. He'd copied down all the details from the notice board before he'd made his way to the End the day before and given them to Maya as soon as she arrived. After her unexpected phone call on Monday night, Joe had thought she would have shown more interest in the details but, after one quick read-through, she'd crumpled up the note and said, "Well, there goes that idea." It had been a bit odd.

"It's on tonight," said Maya quietly.

"Yeah, Wednesday. I remember," Joe nodded again.

"It starts at five o'clock," Maya continued, her super-straight hair bobbing as she walked.

"Uh-huh. And you said yesterday that you wouldn't be able to go because you wouldn't be able to sneak back home before your parents got in from work..." Joe prompted, trying to figure out what she was thinking. He felt all right now; that crushing uncomfortableness had lifted once the conversation had got going.

"That's right. They wouldn't want me to do it because they'd worry that I'd want to keep it up once I start sixth form after summer, and that would *never* do," said Maya bitterly.

"And A-levels mean commitment!" quipped

Joe, remembering the line Maya said her parents were drumming into her.

"Oh, but, Joe – I really *want* to go!" she whimpered, scrunching up her nose like a five-year-old who had been told it was time for bed. It really wasn't a Maya thing to do.

"But what choice have you got? If you reckon your parents would be dead against it..."

"I know! But it's just not fair!"

Joe looked at his friend to check he was with the right person – this sort of whingeing was more up Catrina's street.

"C'mon," he said as they approached the turning that would take them towards the End-of-the-Line café. "Ollie and Sonja will cheer you up. And if they can't, we can always laugh at whatever bizarre thing Cat's squeezed herself into today."

Instead of laughing, as Joe hoped she would, Maya stopped dead in her tracks.

"Sorry, Joe," she said, suddenly breaking into a smile, "I've got other plans."

"Uh, where are you going?" he asked as she turned and headed off down a side street.

"Guess!" she grinned over her shoulder.

"But what about your parents?" he called after her.

"Tough!" she shouted and gave him a wave.

Wow, this is getting weird, thought Joe as he watched Maya stroll away with a super-confident swagger. *Now she's turned into Sonja...*

CHAPTER 4

MAYA JOINS THE CLUB

The sour smell of the chemicals made her catch her breath.

But it was exciting, taking Maya right back to those days at her old school in the city. Art had been her favourite subject and the art class was where she had found her best friends.

And now... now there were no more art classes and no more old friends – Emma, Becky and Sabine had never stayed in touch with Maya once her family had moved to Winstead. They'd started to drift away from her before that, of course, when, subject-wise, Maya had gone down the route of 'all science and serious stuff' as Becky had called it, and they'd stopped being in the same classes.

"Well, that's life," Maya had told herself at the

time, although it hurt her more than anyone knew.

Standing in the doorway of the one-storey, breeze-block-built annexe, she breathed in the pungent smell again and gazed around. There were about half a dozen people pottering around a room that was plastered in an amazing array of mostly black and white prints. Over to the right was another door with an unlit red light above it and the message 'Knock first – or I'll have to kill you!' printed boldly on an A3 sheet of paper. The darkroom, obviously.

"Hi, are you here for the camera club?"

Maya nodded.

"Come on in, then – and shut the door!"

The gruff Glaswegian tones belonged to a tall, lanky guy in his late twenties who stood slightly stooped as if the ceiling was too low for his frame, or as if he was slightly apologetic about his own height.

"I'm Alex," he grinned, bounding over to her. "I teach art here at Downfield. And photography, obviously!"

"I'm Maya – Maya Joshi," she smiled back. At least he seemed friendly.

Despite her show of bravado when she'd left Joe, she'd had a bad case of butterflies as she'd followed the signs to this building. It was hard going somewhere new on your own – but then Maya had done quite a bit of that over the last few years.

"Done any photography before, Maya?"

"Yes, but not for a long time," she answered, thinking back to the mounted prints that she still hadn't found, despite rummaging through every cupboard in the house that morning.

"No worries, it'll soon come back to you. Now let me get your details," said the teacher, walking towards a table and motioning her to a chair.

Scribbling down her name in a jotter, Alex explained more about the club. "You've only missed a couple of meetings; it started at the beginning of the holidays. But it's not just a summer thing – it'll be ongoing. Are you up for that?"

"Yes, I think so," said Maya enthusiastically, before remembering the glitch that was bothering her. "I can't stay for the full two hours though – I have to be home before seven."

"OK," Alex nodded. "Come a bit earlier then, if you like, so you don't miss out. I'm always here setting up well before five o'clock anyway."

"Thanks," she smiled, taking another quick glance round the room and itching to get started.

"Now, here's where we get technical," he smiled. "Have you got your own camera, Maya?"

"Just a cheap instant snap job," she admitted, her heart sinking. She remembered the chunky, professional 35mm camera she'd borrowed from her old school. Her little snapper didn't really compare – and she could see from the slight grimace on the teacher's face that he thought so too.

"It'll do if you haven't got anything else, but obviously, if you can get your hands on something like this..." he leant over and grabbed a Pentax from the worktop, "...it's much better in that you can change lenses and experiment a lot more. There are usually plenty you could borrow from the centre, but unfortunately everyone else got in before you."

"I'll try to get one," said Maya, even though she hadn't a clue how she could manage it.

"Now here's something else I'm going to land on you before I introduce you to the others," said Alex, placing an A4 poster in front of her. 'Peacock Trust Photography Competition' was all Maya managed to read before he continued.

"This competition is being run by the Peacock Gallery to encourage young talent. The theme is 'Informal Portraits', which leaves it quite open."

Maya nodded, glancing down at the flyer again.

"The good news is that there's some excellent

camera equipment as prizes – which is why I want everyone here at the club to enter," Alex continued. "The *bad* news is that the competition closes in less than three weeks' time."

He noted the surprised look on Maya's face and quickly tried to reassure her.

"I know everyone here's had a head start, but you've still got time. Have a think about taking pictures of family and friends. And to help everyone, we're all going on an afternoon field trip next Wednesday – can you make that?"

Maya's mind raced – she'd be babysitting Ravi. What could she do?

"Yes, of course," she said out loud. *I'll worry about it later*, she thought to herself.

"Right, I'll give you details about that before you leave tonight. But let's get you into the swing of things, shall we?"

"Thanks, Mr, er..." Maya stumbled, suddenly realising she hadn't caught his last name.

"Alex – just Alex," he grinned at her. "It's not school, remember!"

Thank God! Maya thought as she smiled back.

As Alex got to his feet, he called across to one of the other people in the room. "Billy?"

"Yep?" answered a boy of about seventeen, looking away from the two girls he'd been talking to.

"Billy – are you ready to go into the darkroom?"

"Sure," said the boy, holding up a roll of film.

"Can you take Maya with you and talk her through the developing process?"

"'Course," he replied, turning his bright blue eyes towards Maya and smiling broadly.

The tiniest shiver fluttered up Maya's back and she was aware of feeling slightly light-headed.

Must be the chemicals in here, she reasoned, standing up to follow Billy into the darkroom.

CHAPTER 5

•••••••••••••••••••••••••••

JOE WOBBLES

"What're you doing Saturday?"

"Going to my dad's, remember?"

Matt furrowed his brow in concentration for a second.

"Oh, yeah, you said something about that earlier in the week, didn't you?"

Joe sighed. There he'd been, pouring his heart out about the situation with his dad on Monday, and Matt hadn't really taken it in. But it was typical Matt behaviour – like Catrina, he was pretty much an airhead when it came to other people's emotions. Also like Catrina, Matt was all too often so wrapped up in himself that there wasn't time to think about anyone else.

Funny it never worked out when the two of them were a couple, Joe mused to himself.

They're a perfect match...

"Well, I've got a better offer," Matt continued blithely. "I've got a job out of town – doing some girl's eighteenth in this big marquee set-up – and I could do with the company."

Joe hesitated. Apart from the obvious difficulty – turning down his dad's very pointed invitation – Matt's first choice of DJ buddy was usually Ollie, with Joe occasionally tagging along for the ride. Ultra-quiet Joe and super-confident Matt didn't do all that much 'solo' pairing up.

"What about Ollie?" Joe asked, then followed Matt's gaze over to where Ollie and Kerry were leaning towards each other over the metal-topped serving counter.

"Isn't it against health and hygiene regulations to snog like that in a café?" Matt grimaced.

"Just 'cause you're jealous of anyone getting a snog," chipped in Sonja, breaking away from her conversation with Cat.

An hour on and the two girls were still talking about Maya's out-of-character turnaround earlier in the evening. They'd pumped Joe for every scrap of detail about her sudden break for freedom – or at least, break for the photography club – but they knew it added up to the same thing as far as Maya was concerned.

"Stay out of my conversation and get back to

your tittle-tattle," smirked Matt. Sonja gave him a light smack across the head.

"I knew that was coming," he grinned at Joe.

"Serves you right, too," Cat cackled. "Getting that big head of yours in the way of Sonja's hand!"

"Well, at least I haven't got a big mouth like yours," Matt sniped back. "Anyway, as I was saying, Joe..."

Joe shifted uncomfortably in his seat – he never knew when Matt and Catrina's jibes were going to turn more barbed, as they had a habit of doing.

"...it seems that Ollie's being a good little boyfriend and babysitting Kerry's brother and daft dog on Saturday night."

"Why?" asked Joe, completely confused.

"Kerry's folks are going out to some dinner party and Kerry already had plans to spend the evening with the ugly sisters here..."

"Hey!" said Cat and Sonja in unison.

"Sorry," Matt apologised, "I meant the ugly *cousins* here..."

He ignored Sonja's second swipe to his head and carried on regardless.

"...so Ollie turned all chivalrous and offered his services as kid and dogsitter. And that's why he can't come."

And that's why I'm second choice, thought Joe. *Ollie's busy so I'll do as the extra pair of hands to help move Matt's gear...*

Not that Joe didn't fancy going to this eighteenth. A chance to hang out at what was probably going to be a brilliant party versus a barely civilised tea with his dad and girlfriend? There wasn't much comparison really. Apart from the promises he'd made...

"I can't come," shrugged Joe.

"'Course you can!" said Matt enthusiastically. "I've got it all figured out! This party, right, is at this big farmhouse just outside that godforsaken little village your dad lives in."

Joe was beginning to see where Matt was coming from.

"So, *you* go out and spend the afternoon with Daddy and play the good little son," Matt explained, "then *I'll* come by about 7.00 pm and whisk you off to Partyville. After that, I drop you off in the early hours and you still have a father-son bonding breakfast together on Sunday!"

"I don't know..." said Joe, apprehensively, even though it sounded like the perfect solution.

"Look, what would you be missing? A night in front of the box watching the Lottery show or whatever, while Daddy and his bird cuddle up on the sofa?"

Matt could be persuasive at the best of times and now he was saying all the right things. If it wasn't for that voice of conscience whispering away in the other ear, Joe would have said yes in a heartbeat.

"Come on..." grinned Matt. "You know you want to."

But you promised your dad... said the righteous voice.

"Whaddya say, Joe?"

...and your mum, it whispered again.

"Why not?" said Joe, suddenly deaf to anything anyone had to say in the head department.

CHAPTER 6

● ●

MAYA GETS A GRILLING

Maya looked over at the clock above the jukebox. Half past six. Then she looked down at her own watch and read the *real* time: 12.30 pm. Good – she still had twenty minutes before she'd have to leave to pick Ravi up.

"I don't know why you even bother looking at that clock," shrugged Cat. "They'd be better off having a sundial in here for accuracy."

"Force of habit," Maya smiled at her. She actually liked the wonky clock at the End-of-the-Line-Café. And the equally wonky jukebox that tricked you by playing songs you'd never requested and at speeds you'd never known existed. And for not working at all, if it didn't feel like it, no matter how much Nick the owner swore at it or kicked it.

For that matter, Maya loved the demented old lady who ran the launderette across the road from the café too. With her own ferociously ordered and time-sensitive life, distractions like Mad Vera doing the cancan between the spin dryers, and the surprise times and tunes that came courtesy of the End's temperamental clock and jukebox, all added a certain sparkle to Maya's day.

"So, I guess you could say last night was a success?" said Sonja, her eyes sparkling. "To think our Maya could be snapping the supermodels of the future for the cover of *Elle* one day!"

"And, of course, if you need any models, I for one would be only too glad to help," said Cat, turning one shoulder coquettishly towards Maya and pouting her Very Berry lips for all she was worth.

"In your dreams, Cat," snapped Sonja, staring at her cousin's peroxide-blonde head of curls. "With that hairstyle, you may fancy yourself as Marilyn Monroe, but with those black roots and big ears, you look more like Minnie Mouse..."

"Ooh, get back in the knife drawer, Miss Sharp!" sniped Cat. "It's my 'theatrical' look, *actually*. And just 'cause you—"

"Stop!" said Maya, holding up her hands in the traditional referee mode she used when it came to Cat and Sonja.

"Sorry, Maya," Sonja apologised, suddenly aware that the bickering was spoiling their friend's moment. "Anyway, you were saying that you want to enter this contest?"

"Yes," nodded Maya, positively beaming and still on a high from the previous evening. "And if you don't mind, I'd like to bring my camera along to the sleepover on Saturday and just, you know, snap whatever happens!"

"Yeah! It'll be a laugh!" said Sonja, turning to Cat. "Won't it?"

"Yes... " Cat responded dubiously. "As long as you promise something..."

Maya looked at her friend and wondered what she was getting at.

"As long as you don't take any pictures of me *after* I've taken my make-up off!"

Before Maya could say anything – let alone imagine Cat completely devoid of her warpaint – Joe wandered in and plonked himself down in the window booth beside the girls.

"All right, Joey?" Sonja grinned at him.

"OK," Joe nodded slightly. He hated being called Joey, but he'd never have let on to anyone.

"Maya was telling us about her photography class last night," Cat began to explain.

"It's not a class, it's a club," corrected Maya, trying to keep the distinction from any kind of school activity absolute and obvious.

"Yeah, yeah, whatever," shrugged Cat, taking a noisy slurp from her Diet Coke.

"Was it good?" asked Joe, turning towards Maya. Last night she'd seemed like a completely different girl to him. He was relieved to see that she appeared to be her old, composed self again.

"Brilliant, thanks," Maya smiled serenely at him.

"And you, uh, got home before your parents, then?" he asked, aware that if that wasn't the case, she wouldn't exactly be saying she'd had a brilliant time.

"Yes, I left early so it wasn't a problem."

"So you'll be going again?" he quizzed her.

"Wait, wait, wait," Sonja interrupted. "No one's asking the important question here."

"Which would be?" Maya asked her friend, wondering what was coming next.

"Which is – how cute was your teacher?"

Maya gasped – she hadn't anticipated this one.

"He's– he's a teacher! He's not fanciable!" she protested.

"Dunno about that," said Cat. "Remember that substitute drama teacher last year – Mr James?"

"Rrrraaaaooooghhhh!" growled Sonja and Cat

in unison, agreed for once on the subject of the cute teacher. For a brief couple of weeks, he had kept the entire female population of both St Mark's school and sixth-form college well entertained in the drooling department.

"Alex isn't like that!" Maya protested again.

"Ooh, *Alex*, is it? How *very* friendly," teased Cat, raising her eyebrows at Sonja.

"It's not school – it's an adult education centre! Alex is what everyone calls him!"

Joe felt for Maya: she wasn't used to being teased like this and she wasn't handling it very well.

"Yeah, OK – Alex it is," nodded Sonja with a straight face. Then a wicked grin spread across her face she added, "And is Alex cute, then?"

"No!" Maya found herself squeaking. "He's just an ordinary bloke!"

"Are you *sure*, Maya?" cut in Cat, following Sonja's lead.

"Yes! Of course! I mean he's not cute like—" she paused before she got in any deeper with her friends, but it was too late.

"Not cute like who?" prodded Sonja.

"Not like... like Billy."

"Billy!" shrieked Sonja and Cat. "Who's Billy?"

Joe couldn't take much more of this. Watching Maya wilt under the other girls' questioning made his toes curl, but he was no match for the combined might of Sonja and Cat. So he kept his mouth shut and his thoughts to himself.

It was a relief at that moment to spot Nick, owner of the End-of-the-Line café, beckoning him over to the counter.

"'Scuse me," Joe said to none of the girls in particular as he rose up from his seat and walked over to Nick, who was decked out in his favourite Kiss T-shirt (recently bought to replace his old Kiss T-shirt).

"Joe – have you got a job this summer?" asked Nick.

"Nope," Joe answered. *If I had, what would I be doing sitting in the café at lunchtime on a Thursday?* he thought to himself.

"How do you fancy helping out here with a few shifts?" said Nick, smoothing his T-shirt down over his ample belly. Joe wondered absently if he'd kept buying the same size top as his very *first* Kiss T-shirt, which was many years and many gallons of beer ago. "The staff, y'know – they all want to take holidays and that."

How inconsiderate of them, thought Joe wryly. But Nick's poor management skills didn't matter that much to Joe – not when it meant the chance of some extra dosh for the summer.

"No problem, Nick."

"Cool. You want to come in on Monday and cover the lunchtime shift, just serving and that?"

"No problem," Joe repeated. He'd never served in a café before, but it didn't bother him. He spent so much time in here with his friends that he probably knew the score as much as any of the staff did.

And anyway, he'd covered for Ollie a couple of times when Ollie was supposed to be manning Nick's second-hand record shop next door – not that Nick had ever found out.

"Right, it's a deal, mate," said Nick, holding out his hand to Joe.

"Right," agreed Joe, wincing from Nick's crushing handshake and turning back to the girls in the window booth.

"Is Nick all right?" hissed Cat theatrically as Joe sat down.

"Yeah – why wouldn't he be?" asked Joe, wondering what on earth Cat meant, grabbing a serviette and wiping smears of egg off the hand that Nick had shaken.

"I just thought he might be a bit, y'know, down."

"Why?" Joe asked again.

"Because..." whispered Cat, with an ear-to-ear wicked grin, "my mum chucked him last night!"

"Really!" gasped Sonja. "Well, I'll say this for

them – they lasted longer than any of us thought!"

"Yeah, but we all bet that it wouldn't last past the weekend when we found out about it!" Joe chipped in, then immediately felt self-conscious joking about the subject.

It had been a laugh a month or so back when they'd all found out about ageing rocker Nick dating Cat's super-efficient, super-elegant, super-uptight mum. But it was also around then that Cat had got herself in a real mess emotionally – spreading loads of lies that nearly ruined the crowd's easygoing relationship with Nick, and nearly split up Ollie and Kerry too...

But look at her now, thought Joe, gazing in wonder at Cat, who was filling everyone in with the gory details of the bust-up as though nothing had ever happened. As though she didn't realise how lucky she was that everyone, especially Kerry, Ollie and Nick, had shrugged off the whole episode.

She bounces back faster than a rubber ball, that one, Joe mused before another thought occurred to him. *But then she's an expert at hiding things...*

Not for the first time, Joe stared at Cat, seeing past the superficial, silly and often selfish side of her, casting his mind back a couple of months to the time she'd confronted him, when he was bingeing on booze, and told him the truth about why her father had left them years before. About her dad's alcoholism and how he'd deserted his own daughter, without a backward glance, without a second thought. Joe had already known the trouble he was in, but Cat's confession was the reality check he'd needed to get back on track.

"...and *she* said, 'I'm sorry, Nick, but that's my decision and it's final' – like she was at a board meeting or something! And then I heard her slam the phone down."

"Hey, Cat, check it out..." said Sonja, nodding in the direction of the counter, where Nick was singing along to the Oasis track belting out of the jukebox and polishing up some glasses. "He doesn't exactly look heartbroken."

"Probably knows what a lucky escape he had from my dragon – sorry – mother," quipped Cat.

"Probably didn't have the courage to finish it himself in case Auntie Sylvia kneecapped him with her office stapler or something," Sonja joined in.

Suddenly aware of how much time had passed, Maya took a quick look at her watch again and pulled on her jacket. "Love to stay and hear more about the romance-that-never-was, but I've got a little brother to pick up."

"Now, Miss Joshi," said Sonja sternly, wagging her finger at Maya, "just because we got sidetracked with the whole Nick'n'Sylvia fiasco, don't go thinking you've got away with not telling us all about this Billy bloke."

"Too right!" piped up Cat, her yellow-blonde curls twirling as she bobbed her head in agreement. "I've never heard you say you fancy anyone – ever!"

"I don't *fancy* him!" Maya protested uselessly. She knew she was on a loser in the face of her two friends' enthusiasm about her supposed love-life. "I just said he seemed kind of... nice, that's all."

"Well if you're keen on this lad, we're here to give you as much advice as we can. Aren't we, Cat?" Sonja raised her eyebrows at her cousin.

"Absolutely!"

Joe looked at Maya's troubled expression. That was obviously what she was worried about.

CHAPTER 7

• •

JOE GETS GALLANT

The puffy white clouds were spinning above him in a circle. It made him feel slightly sick, but he liked the effect too much to stop.

Suddenly, a badly placed knee in his groin made him gasp and a small face loomed into view, obliterating the blue sky above him.

"Joe!" mouthed the gap-toothed, beaming boy. Joe couldn't hear anything over the blare of his Walkman, but he could lip-read his own name well enough.

Sitting bolt upright and hanging on to the kid who'd scrambled over him, Joe used his free hand to yank off his headphones and glance around.

The old painted wooden roundabout creaked round to give him a full 360-degree view of the surrounding park and playground before it came to Maya, who waved and said "Hi!" as Joe and Ravi spun slowly past.

Still slightly breathless with pain, Joe stuck his foot out and dragged it along the ground, slowing the roundabout to a standstill.

"Ravi, you've got to take more care! Poor Joe!" Maya admonished her little brother, making an apologetic face at her friend, whose discomfort was obvious.

"It's OK," Joe lied, ruffling Ravi's almost black hair. "What are you two up to?"

"Working off some of his excess energy before I hand him over to Brigid," smiled Maya, sitting next to the boys on the now stationary kiddy-park ride. "I tell you, he's got X-ray eyes – he spotted it was you lying on here from miles away."

"You looked like a drunk man lying down like that," said Ravi matter-of-factly.

Joe cringed inwardly; he did have a vague memory of lying here watching the stars weave together in the sky, in the middle of some alcohol-fuelled whirl in the not-so-distant past.

"Or dead," added Ravi.

"OK, enough, Rav," said Maya firmly. "Sorry – he's going through a bit of a macabre stage at the moment. But I have to say, it's just as well there's no one in the playpark at the moment or you might have got some suspicious looks."

"I didn't think of that," Joe admitted. "We've usually been here in the evenings, haven't we? Like when the fair was last here."

"Yes, when the children who this place is *meant* for are safely tucked up in bed, you big kid," she teased him gently.

"What *were* you doing, Joe?" asked Ravi, staring earnestly into Joe's face.

Joe was too embarrassed to explain what he was listening to on his personal stereo and so told the boy only half the story.

"Uh, I was just seeing what the clouds look like from this angle, Rav..." he shrugged. Ravi looked at him for a second, then up at the sky.

"Brilliant!" he said, clambering off Joe and flopping down on his back on the hard wooden surface. "Spin me round, will you, Joey? Huh, Joey?"

Maya noticed her friend wince suddenly and wondered why. She said nothing and lifted her feet up on to the running board so that Joe could gently push them off.

"Not too fast or he'll just get sick," she whispered to Joe. He nodded back.

"No I won't!" came a determined voice. "Make it go faster, Joey!"

Shaking her head at Joe, Maya mouthed the word "Don't!" at him.

"OK, Ravi, I'll go a bit faster," said Joe, winking at Maya. "On one condition..."

"What?" piped up Ravi, excitedly.

Joe bent over the seven-year-old and whispered conspiratorially, "As long as you don't call me 'Joey', OK? That kind of bugs me."

"OK," Ravi whispered back, grinning a wide, fat grin back up at his sister's friend.

Maya pretended she hadn't heard.

"So, what were you listening to?" she asked as Joe straightened up and turned his attention back to her. Nothing ever got past Maya and Joe didn't try to make anything up.

"Er, it's just a tape of some rough tracks of the band's," he muttered.

At least that was true – he didn't want to be too specific and have to explain that it was a track he'd written in the spring. The one he'd written about Kerry... No one but Ollie knew that he wrote songs. And no one at all knew how much he liked Kerry.

"Anything I've heard?" Maya asked. She'd been to the few gigs Ollie and Joe's band – The Loud – had played so far.

"Nah – just some new stuff we haven't done yet."

"So when are you guys getting the band together again?"

"Dunno," shrugged Joe. It was a sore point between him and Ollie. They'd talked about advertising for some new band members ages ago, but Ollie seemed to find excuses to put it off every time Joe brought it up lately.

"Is the band taking second place to what's going on between him and Kerry, then?" Maya asked astutely.

"I guess," Joe shrugged again. He didn't want to moan about his best mate's relationship in case it sounded like sour grapes. Which it was. *And some...*

"I know Ollie and Kerry are all over each other, but they'll come back down to earth soon and remember the rest of us, I'm sure," said Maya, very wisely for someone who'd never had a boyfriend. But then, Maya was pretty wise about most things.

Apart from maybe her own life, thought Joe, remembering her confessions from earlier in the week.

"Yeah, I reckon you're right," he agreed, stepping foot over foot, keeping up the slow rotation of the roundabout.

"Oh, I meant to ask – what was Nick after yesterday when he called you over?" asked Maya, referring to their lunchtime rendezvous in the End.

"Not much," said Joe, although he was well chuffed with his job offer. "He asked me to come in and help out at the End. Y'know – holiday cover and that."

"That's great!" exclaimed Maya. "Why didn't you tell us yesterday?"

"Couldn't get a word in edgeways, could I?" grinned Joe.

"I know what you mean," said Maya ruefully. "Between tearing into Nick's love-life and, well, my *non*-love-life, Sonja and Cat were too busy for anything else."

"Anyway, I was glad to hear that you're really keen on that, um, *thing* you went to the other night," Joe said, sensing that Maya might prefer the subject changed, but aware that she might not want the photography club mentioned out loud in front of her brother if it was some big family secret. "It sounded good."

"I think it will be," Maya smiled at him, appreciative of his subtlety. "I think it might be just what I need right now. I've really, really missed doing something artistic, you know what I mean?"

Joe nodded. The thought of not writing songs freaked him out. And he couldn't imagine what it would be like to have parents who were as strict as Maya's, to stop you doing the subjects you really loved. For a second, he breathed a sigh of relief for his ordinary, kind mum, even though she sometimes drove him mad with her clinginess.

"The only problem is," said Maya, a troubled look crossing her face, "I don't really have a proper camera."

"What – like one of those big chunky jobs with the kind of lens you swivel?" Joe asked, picturing the black and silver Konica belonging to his dad that he used to marvel over when he was young.

"Yes, that's right. The club had some to lend out, but I joined too late – they'd all been snapped up."

"Don't worry," said Joe, an idea coming to him. Doing this photography thing was really important to Maya – that was obvious – and Joe wanted to help her make it happen. "I could get you one! Like a long-term loan – to get you started!"

"But how?" asked Maya.

Before Joe could answer, a small voice piped up.

"Maya, I feel sick..."

CHAPTER 8

● ●

'JOEY' GRITS HIS TEETH

Joe stepped off the bus, looked around the quaint village square and sighed. It was like arriving in Postman Pat land.

Apart from the toytown-sized houses that lined the four sides of the square, a gift shop and café vied to outdo each other in cutesy appeal: lacy, scallop-edged curtains and dainty knick-knacks adorned both windows.

Bit like Dad's place, snorted Joe as he hauled his sports bag up on to his shoulder and stomped down the turning that led to his father's bungalow.

Much as he'd rather have been anywhere else this weekend, the one thing Joe was glad of was that he'd managed to persuade his dad to let him make his own way there. His father had been determined to pick him up from his mother's, which no doubt would have meant Gillian twittering away for the full forty-minute journey, and Joe couldn't have stood that torture.

Coming alongside the bungalow's flower-festooned garden, he found his feet dragging as if they were weighed down with sandbags.

Here we go, he told himself. *Just say yes, no and smile a bit and it'll all be over. Until the next time I'm forced to come...*

"Joey! Yoo-hoo!"

A smiling, plumpish young woman in gardening gloves appeared out of a clump of something blossomy.

"Uh, hello, um..."

Try as he might, Joe couldn't ever manage to say her name out loud. It had been four years since his dad had hooked up with Gillian, but it hadn't got any easier to think of her as permanent enough to warrant common name usage. 'Her' or 'your girlfriend' was the best he could do when he talked to his father.

"Bobby! Oh, Bobbyyyyy! Joey's here!" she trilled to no one in particular.

And that was another thing that grated. First, he was Joe – not Joey, and second, when had his dad ever been 'Bobby'?

Robert, that's what everyone else calls him;

that's the only name he's ever answered to before – before her, thought Joe sullenly, remembering how much his father had hated to have his name shortened, back in his old life. *Before she turned him into some juvenile, love-sick puppy...*

"Joey! Well, hello!" said his father cheerfully, appearing from the side of the house and wiping his hands on his jeans. "We've been looking out for you – thought you might be here on the earlier bus!"

"Don't do that, Bobby, sweetie! Those are clean on!" Gillian chided Joe's father good-naturedly before Joe could respond. Not that he could have come up with a good answer; his only excuse being that he'd lain in bed, dreading the impending visit so much that he'd been unable to bring himself to get up in time.

"Oh, Gilly—"

Gilly! cringed Joe. *Can this get any more nauseating?*

"Don't fuss! It's only a bit of flour!" his father bantered back affectionately. "Mexican tonight, Joey? Fancy that?"

Closing the metal garden gate behind him, Joe nodded vaguely. Here was yet another thing – apart from the new name. His dad had become a 'new man' since he'd hooked up with 'Gilly', doing his fair share of housekeeping and positively relishing his new responsibility in the kitchen department.

"Come on in! Let me take that!" his dad jollied Joe along, lifting the bag from his back. "Been a while, hasn't it, mate?"

"Mmmm," nodded Joe, wincing inside.

Don't call me mate, he said deep inside his head. *Don't act like we're all lads together or something. Like I should understand why you should prefer this rosy, rural lifestyle with the Cabbage Patch Doll to life with me and Mum...*

"How's, er, your mum?"

Like you care, thought Joe, following his father through to the kitchen.

"OK, I guess," Joe shrugged.

"So," Robert Gladwin continued, slightly self-consciously, "I thought we could have a really nice meal together tonight. You know, just the three of us...?"

"Uh, yeah," nodded Joe, pulling out a kitchen chair (complete with home-made gingham cushion tie-on) from beneath the shiny pine table. "But the thing is, I've got something on later."

"Oh."

Joe could clearly see the look of disappointment on his father's face and felt a sudden rush of pleasure at being able to inflict that on him.

"What... what have you got planned, then?" his father asked, in an unconvincingly casual manner.

"My mate, Matt – you don't know him – he's DJing at a party near here and I'm going to give him a hand."

"What time will you have to be off?" said Gillian, joining them in the kitchen, hearing the exchange as she came through the hall.

"Matt'll be round to pick me up about seven," Joe answered her, aware of Gillian rubbing his father's back, the way a mother would comfort a child who'd broken his favourite toy.

What's the big deal with this? Joe wondered. *What the hell were we going to find to talk to each other about all evening anyway?*

● ● ●

"Right, time to get the tea on!" his dad said brightly.

It had been a long, painfully uncomfortable afternoon, spent in the trellis-infested beer garden of Ye Old Boare Inn.

And boy was it full of old bores, thought Joe as they arrived back at the bungalow. His dad – the biggest bore of them all, as far as Joe was concerned – had spent the afternoon introducing him proudly to all the other yuppies who'd swapped town and city life for their sanitised version of country living.

The only stilted topics of conversation when they'd been on their own – with giggling Gillian, of course – was college (not a great subject to dwell on during the holidays) and what Joe wanted for his upcoming birthday. All Joe really wanted was to leap back in space and time to a point where Gillian had never come to work for his father and therefore hadn't caused his parents to split up. But as this was an impossibility, Joe simply shrugged and said he didn't know.

"I'm just going to change my T-shirt," he mumbled, hoping to while away a few minutes bumbling around in the guest bedroom. (*"Your room!"* Gillian had gushed when Joe had first visited them at their new home a couple of years previously.) Joe was grateful for *anything* that helped tick away time on this pointless visit.

Rummaging in the sports bag that sat at the foot of the spare bed, Joe pulled out a clean but crushed, plain navy V-necked top. Yanking off the old top and sliding on the new one, he caught sight of himself in the oval gilt mirror that hung above the chest of drawers.

I look like a sulky thirteen-year-old, Joe grimaced, recognising the pained, angry expression that had become a fixture around the time his parents had separated. He'd hated the way he felt at that time – deserted, confused, full of wordless fury – and he hated now to see echoes of the old, miserable Joe all over again.

Joe knew he was never destined to be a happy-go-lucky, laid-back type – that wouldn't have changed even if his parents hadn't split up – but he liked the person he was now a whole lot more than that miserable thirteen-year-old. And all that was down to his friends and their acceptance of him and all his shy, awkward ways.

Ollie... well, Ollie had always been there – right from sandpit and see-saw days – but the real turning point was when they'd hooked up with the girls three summers ago.

Ollie and Joe had begun to hang out regularly at Nick's café, and so had Sonja, Cat and Kerry, whom the boys had vaguely known at school. After a few amiable arguments over who got to sit in the window booth, they'd compromised and shared the table – and a friendship – ever since.

Then along came Maya, followed by Matt last year. They – along with his mum – were his family now. He belonged with them, not this man he felt nothing for and his silly, empty-headed girlfriend.

Rubbing his face with his hands, as if that might help erase the hateful expression, Joe was suddenly struck with an idea that might take up another chunk of time...

He thought for a second about where and how his father kept things around the house, then decided that – despite his new image – his dad was a creature of habit.

Crossing the hall – with a quick glance to check there was no one around – he slowly pushed open the door to his father's bedroom. He gave a cursory, dismissive glance at the pile of soft toys that languished in the middle of the floral duvet and made his way over to the fitted wardrobe.

Opening one sliding door, Joe was met by a crush of floral clothes that seemed to match the bedspread: Gillian's stuff. He stretched his neck and scanned the top shelf, but could only make out more folded clothes in sugary pastel shades, plus some kind of rolled up, quilted blanket with what looked like the alphabet and clowns on it.

God, how old is this woman? Twenty-six going on five? Joe scoffed, sliding the door closed with a dull thud.

He drew the other door open – jeans, cords, some brightly coloured shirts he hadn't seen before and some work suits that seemed very familiar. Standing on his toes, Joe reached up and began to rummage in the jumble of old shoeboxes that were stored up on the top shelf, just as they had been back at the house in Winstead.

Aha! Joe said to himself as his fingers collided with cool metal in a box at the back. *Bingo!*

"Need a hand there, Joey?" said a soft voice.

Joe whipped round to see Gillian standing at the door of the bedroom, gazing questioningly at him. With her light brown curly hair, round dimpled face and keen-to-please smile, she suddenly reminded him of someone.

"Er, I was– I was just—" He scrambled for words, feeling beads of sweat break out instantaneously on his forehead. "Um, looking for a jumper or sweatshirt or something to borrow for tonight. In case it's cold later on. I, uh, didn't bring a jacket with me."

Lame, lame, lame, he chastised himself, holding the heavy camera out of sight behind his back.

"I see," Gillian smiled encouragingly at him, but he could sense her eyes flickering from his face to his sides. Had she seen him take the Konica? Was she going to say anything?

Lifting her shoulders in an almost imperceptible shrug, Gillian said, "Right, then. Coming through? Kettle's on..."

She *had* spotted what he was up to, Joe was pretty sure, but he sensed that she wasn't about to say anything. To his dad or to him.

She doesn't want the hassle of a confrontation. *She just wants everything to be 'nice'*, thought Joe, getting a handle on her character.

In a flash, he knew why she seemed so familiar all of a sudden: she was exactly like a much younger version of his own mother.

CHAPTER 9

● ●

SYMPATHY SLEEPOVER

"I don't think I suit blue," said Maya warily, examining her new look, courtesy of Catrina and her toolbox of make-up.

"'Course you do!" Cat exclaimed, standing back in her silky plum pyjamas and proudly admiring her handiwork.

"Yeah, it's brilliant!" chipped in Sonja positively, although Cat's trademark Very Berry lipstick and over-the-top eyeshadow didn't sit too well on Maya's light brown complexion. And her thick, glossy dark hair hadn't responded very enthusiastically to the curls Cat had tried to sculpt in with her portable steam tongs.

Maya glanced over at Kerry in the hope of an honest response.

"Mmm!" squeaked Kerry non-committally.

She'd always envied Sonja's Scandinavian, glowing good looks, and she knew that Cat's in-yer-face glamour always got the boys drooling, but Maya's naturally beautiful, minimally made-up face was the one she was most in awe of. Possibly not the way it looked tonight, though.

"Listen, Maya, this is all for your own good," said Sonja, rifling through the mound of chocolate and discarded wrappers in the middle of the rug for an elusive Crunchie mini-bar. "Gorgeous as you are, you need to start experimenting; expanding your options, now that you're into the idea of shaking up your life."

"*And* now that *Billy's* on the scene!" Cat purred mischievously.

"Look, I've *told* you," Maya started, half irritated, half amused by their teasing. "I've only met him once—"

"In a cosy darkroom!" interrupted Cat, her eyes wide and suggestive.

"—and he seemed kind of cute! End of story!"

"Well, you may protest, but Cat's got a point," Sonja nodded sagely, a smile playing on her lips. It was good to see Maya *almost* having a laugh – she'd seemed so stressed out earlier in the week. "After all, we've never heard you say you thought anyone was cute before!"

"And it's time you had a boyfriend – it's

ridiculous to think of a girl being sixteen and never having been out with anyone," said Cat through a mouthful of salt and vinegar crisps, getting seriously stuck into the nibbles now that her hard work was done.

"And it's amazing how many boys some sixteen-year-old girls have been out with," Sonja jibed back at her, referring to Catrina's sizeable list of exes. "Don't you think so, Maya?"

She turned to Maya, who was sitting cross-legged on the bed wearing a pair of crisp, navy and white gingham PJs, a mirror in one hand and an overstuffed, fluffy polar bear – who normally lived on the spare bed – gripped defensively to her chest. Maya managed a nod and wriggled her nose up at her reflection.

"You're just jealous, Son! When was the last time *you* had a boyfriend?" Cat couldn't help but dig.

Sonja shot her a withering glance. So, she hadn't been out with anyone for the last... however long, but *her* life wasn't the issue here. Cat seemed to be in danger of straying away from the main focus of tonight: Maya.

After her out-of-character outburst and behaviour this week, the other three girls had agreed that they'd use the sleepover to encourage Maya to talk about her situation at home, if that's what she wanted (Kerry's suggestion). They'd spoken about giving her a make-over to cheer her up (Cat's suggestion). They'd planned to tell her to just go and snog the face off this Billy lad, if she really liked him (definitely Cat's suggestion).

Sonja reached for the nearest chocolate bar without looking, tore off the wrapper and bit through the chocolate into... coconut.

Yuk! Sweetened cardboard... Sonja thought to herself, grimacing. She swallowed quickly (without chewing), shuffled the half-munched bar back into the pile and leant over to the music system to change the soppy ballad compilation that Kerry had stuck on to something a bit more upbeat. Since she'd fallen in love, Kerry's taste in music had definitely taken a slushy turn for the worse.

"Hey, listen, here's your horoscope, Maya – let's see if you've got some good stuff coming!" said Cat, flipping through the pages of a magazine.

That's more like it, thought Sonja. Cat could always be relied upon to be totally aware of her own strengths and weaknesses, and knew without a shadow of a doubt that – compared to Sonja and Kerry – she was completely rubbish at being sympathetic. At least with the horoscope thing she was *trying* to be helpful.

Rifling through a pile of tapes, Sonja found something she liked, stuck it in the tape deck and pressed the rewind button. As she waited for the counter to whirr back to zero, she stood up and walked over to the padded velvet window seat, half-listening to Cat's voice enthusiastically spelling out Maya's future. She could make a fortune in TV ad voice-overs, that was for sure.

"*Libra. Your life's been in a rut, but now you're brave enough to start looking for new challenges...*"

Sonja's bedroom was fantastic, like the rest of the house. She had a huge upstairs room and a view of the tops of the trees way over in the park, several streets away. And even now in the twilight, Sonja could make out the last red rays of the sun clinging to the darkened branches.

She jumped slightly as the tape deck on her music system clunked to a halt. Striding over, Sonja leant down and pressed play.

"*...which just might include meeting a new love*," continued Cat theatrically, "*without you even trying!*"

Sonja plonked herself back down next to Kerry, who was sitting on the rug, hugging her knees, eyes wide, completely absorbed in listening to Maya's horoscope.

Look at Kerry lapping this stuff up – now that

she's so wrapped up in Ollie, she wants everyone to be in love! thought Sonja, gazing fondly at her best friend. *That's if she doesn't put us all off any kind of romance by going on and on about him all the time, like she's been doing lately...*

"Oh!" exclaimed Kerry as the opening bars of a song came on. "Is this that *Best Album in the World* compilation? This is one of Ollie's favourites!"

"Uh-huh," muttered Sonja, trying to ignore her. "Hey, Maya – I saw your darling sister Sunny in the End late this afternoon, with a bunch of mates. They were all showing off something rotten. Looked like they were driving Anna completely mad."

Maya rolled her eyes. "That'll be all her acting buddies from summer school – they were having a rehearsal for some play this afternoon."

"Getting worse, is she?" asked Cat. Ravi they all knew and loved – like Kerry's little brother Lewis – but Sunita hadn't endeared herself to any of the crowd. There was something a bit too cocky about her, a bit too knowing. And a bit too manipulative, the way she twisted her parents round her little finger, while Maya got all the strict treatment.

"Too right," nodded Maya. "She used to be just this annoying kid, but now she's acting all grown up and – I don't know – more *calculating*, somehow."

"Like how?" asked Kerry. Only having the lovable Lewis around, she couldn't imagine what it would be like to live with an annoying sister like Sunny.

"Well, when she was younger, she was a pain in the neck. But now she just..." Maya shook her head, trying to put her thoughts into words. "She just seems to be watching me all the time. Like she's hoping I'll make a mistake or mess up. Like she's somehow in competition with me."

"Do your parents notice?" Cat asked, stunning everyone with a pertinent question.

"No," smiled Maya. "I'm the oldest so I get the grief. Sunny and Ravi can do no wrong as far as they're concerned."

Suddenly, Sonja decided that there was no point in beating about the bush. "So, Maya – that stuff you were going on about earlier this week – about your parents. How long have you been feeling like that?"

Maya seemed to freeze as she continued to look in the mirror. She shrugged, then turned to gaze at her friends. She seemed about to say something.

Instead, to everyone's surprise – including her own – two big fat tears rolled down her cheeks.

"Have some chocolate!" said Cat in alarm and for want of anything more useful to say.

"N-no I couldn't," Maya sniffed, trying to regain her composure.

"Go on, have the last Mars Bar."

Maya shook her head, which made her dark hair fall forward in a soft, chaotic tangle.

"What about some crisps, then?"

"Leave it, Cat," said Sonja, gazing at Maya, whose bottom lip was looking worryingly wobbly. She stood up and sat next to her friend on the bed, putting a comforting arm around her. "This isn't like you, Maya!"

Maya looked at her and shook her head, trying to give Sonja a wry smile. A bubble of snot appeared at her nose.

"Tissue, Cat," Sonja ordered, holding her hand out. "So what's brought this on?"

"Guilt!" shrugged Maya.

"How do you mean?" asked Kerry, gathering up the voluminous white material of her new sleeveless cotton nightshirt – she'd treated herself when she'd been keeping Maya company out shopping that afternoon – and shuffled closer to the bed.

"I can't win!" Maya began to explain as she dabbed her nose with the tissue. "I feel miserable because my parents are so strict that I feel like I'm suffocating, and then when I find something that cheers me up – like the idea of getting into photography – I feel guilty!"

"What for?" asked Cat, who thought feeling guilty was a waste of energy, even though she'd done plenty of things she should feel guilty about in the past.

"Guilty for keeping it from them!"

"But, Maya, do you really think your parents *would* freak out about this photography business?" Sonja quizzed her. She'd met Maya's parents plenty of times and they'd always been pleasantly polite, if not quite warm and friendly, to her and the others. It was upsetting to think that they were making Maya so unhappy – whether they knew it or not. "You could promise that it wouldn't interfere with your school stuff once term starts up again, couldn't you?"

"No, I'd never get away with it – they'd think it was a waste of time. My parents like to know my life runs to a tight timetable. They already think they're being very fair, letting me hang out with you guys at weekends and stuff..."

"Well, so you'll have to keep your class a secret from them – but it's not like you're robbing a bank or something! I mean, it's not worth beating yourself up about it, is it?" Sonja reasoned.

"But it's not just having to lie about the photography club, is it?" said Maya agitatedly. By now, she was clutching a pillow to her chest too, smothering the polar bear that was still in her arms. A spot of black plastic nose peeked pathetically over the downy bundle, as if searching for air. "I have to lie *all* the time, just to have a bit of freedom. It's not as if *you* all go around lying to your families, is it?"

"Well, no," Sonja conceded. Her parents were cool about everything and trusted her implicitly. There was no reason to lie.

"I never see my mother often enough to lie to her," shrugged Cat. "And when we *do* run into each other around the flat, we tend to concentrate our energies into good, solid, slanging matches."

Kerry gulped and pushed her specs up her nose. She didn't want to think about this issue too hard: her mum had given her a now-you-and-Ollie-aren't-getting-too-serious-are-you? talk a couple of nights previously, and Kerry – knowing exactly what her mother was trying to get at – had assured her that nothing was further from her mind.

Which wasn't strictly true: all too often recently, Kerry found herself wondering what it would be like to sleep with Ollie. Not that she was about to or anything, but...

"Coffee, anyone?" she squeaked, keen to slip out of the room before anyone spotted her own tell-tale guilty look.

• • •

"You know your trouble, Maya...?"

Sonja paused for a minute as she saw Kerry struggle round the bedroom door, kneeing it open awkwardly. Her nightshirt had twisted itself unhelpfully around her legs and she was splashing coffee all over the tray.

Kerry stopped mid-wobble and looked at the scene in front of her. The mattress had been pulled off Sonja's bed, as well as the one from the spare bed, and both now lay on the floor, along with another mattress snaffled from somewhere else in the house, and an inflated Lilo. (Sonja had said earlier that they'd draw straws for who was going to sleep on that, but Kerry had a sinking feeling that she knew who that someone would be.) They'd been positioned into a cross shape in the middle of the room, with a small, square space left in the middle, filled with the debris of the choc-a-thon.

Sonja, Maya and Cat lay facing each other, stomach-down (on the three mattresses, Kerry wasn't surprised to notice), obviously continuing the Maya Salvation Meeting from a more relaxed position.

"Stick the tray down here, Kerry, and come and join us," said Sonja, first brushing aside the chocolate remains in between them all and then motioning towards the duvet-covered Lilo. She coughed, ready to restart her speech.

"Didn't you bring any biscuits?" Cat interrupted, turning to Kerry.

"No," Kerry answered in a voice that got about as irritated as she ever showed, which wasn't much. The Lilo farted and squelched as she tried to get comfy.

"*Right,*" Sonja said firmly, trying to get their attention. Sonja was herself a fast-food junkie, but she was always amazed at Cat's ability to eat non-stop. "As I was saying... Maya, your trouble is that you're *way* smarter than all of us put together. In fact, you're so smart that you've been able to hide how miserable you've been feeling. But in the end, that's not very smart, is it? Just bottling it up like that?"

Maya was still clinging to the polar bear, using him now as a pillow, half of him squashed under her chest, half under her chin. His beady little glass eyes, staring slightly cross-eyed at Sonja, looked ready to pop out.

"I guess you're right..."

"'Course she is," Cat agreed as she rummaged through the empty wrappers on the floor with her long, manicured fingernails.

"*And* you're too serious," Sonja continued. "I think what you need is—"

"Hey, who's eaten half this Bounty?" Cat butted in, waving the half-chomped chocolate bar in the air.

"—is a really brilliant night out, with just us girls," finished Sonja, skipping over Cat's comment.

"What do you mean, exactly? What kind of night out?" said Cat, throwing the rejected chocolate over her shoulder.

"I *mean* dancing, flirting, having a right laugh..."

"Well, we do that at Matt's often enough, at his parties," said Cat, licking her fingers.

"No, I'm speaking about being really silly – going out to a tacky nightclub, like Enigma."

"That would be a laugh!" snorted Cat.

"Enigma? That club down by the bus station?" said Maya, perking up. "I've never been there."

"Yeah, Maya," Kerry pointed out excitedly, "think about what your horoscope said at the end..."

She scrabbled through the chocolate wrappers and rediscovered the magazine.

"*'And a night out with friends could be full of surprises!'* It's perfect!"

"God, that's amazing!" said Cat enthusiastically.

Maya tried to shake her head. She was normally pretty cynical about horoscopes, but her eyes, showing a glint or three, gave her away.

"Right, that's it – it's in the stars... whatever. We're going out," Sonja announced. "Next Friday. No excuses!"

As the other three giggled and cheered – even Maya in a moment of forgetfulness – Sonja smiled an all-conquering smile and subtly slid the magazine under the mattress she was lying on.

There was no point in spoiling the mood by letting any of the others spot that the magazine was dated November last year and was only about eight months out of date...

CHAPTER 10

• •

TROUBLE IN STORE

"Don't look now."

Joe panicked and glanced all around for whatever drama was headed their way.

"Joey! I said not to look!" hissed Matt. "Now, face me and pretend we're having a normal conversation."

Joe stared blankly at Matt, who was nodding in time to the track he was playing on the turntable and mouthing something at him.

"What?" said Joe. "I can't hear you!"

Matt rolled his eyes up to the ceiling in despair.

"I wasn't saying anything, Joey – I was *pretending* to talk!"

"Why?" asked Joe, now completely thrown.

"Because I wanted us to look casual so that these two girls who are coming over will think we haven't noticed them!" Matt explained through gritted teeth.

"What girls?" asked Joe, spinning around involuntarily and finding himself looking straight into two giggling faces.

Thank God they put the lights down in here... he thought to himself, feeling the furnace of a hot flush burn his cheeks and being at least in some small way glad that the extent of his blushing wouldn't be too visible.

Both girls stood grinning stupidly at the boys, then gave each other sly I-know-what-*you're*-thinking looks. These two, decked out almost identically in foxy little black numbers, were obviously the type of best mates who dressed, as well as thought and acted, in unison.

"Hi!" bleated the girls together.

"Hi!" grinned Matt, doing a mock bow to the pair.

"Hi!" chorused the girls again.

Joe managed half a smile and a nod.

"So, you're the DJ?" said one of the Hi! Twins, leaning over and smiling a slightly drunken smile at Matt.

"Sure am," said Matt, smooth as ever.

Well, what else would he be, standing behind this desk and putting records on for the past hour? thought Joe. *A rocket scientist?*

"Fancy a dance?" continued Hi! Twin Number One, flopping her crossed arms down on to Matt's metal record box and giving him – deliberately or not – an eagle's eye view down the front of her strappy, black sequinned dress.

She could give Cat a run for her money, thought Joe, watching Hi! Twin One give it the full-flirt hair toss.

"Can't," shrugged Matt good-naturedly.

"Oh, why not?" said Hi! Twin One, sticking her bottom lip out like a petulant six-year-old.

"I'm the DJ. Got to play the records, y'know?"

Both the Hi! Twins burst into tinny giggles.

"What about you?"

Joe jerked in surprise – he hadn't expected to suddenly be the focus of attention.

"Wha– what?" he stammered.

"If he's the DJ, what are you?" said Hi! Twin Two, tossing her matching shoulder-length hair. She was pretty, but was wearing a ton of – slightly smudged – make-up, Joe realised, looking at her saccharine-pink lips and powdery layer of foundation. Just as with Cat, he had this almost overwhelming urge to scrape some of it off with a fingernail, just for the thrill of seeing bare skin underneath.

"Me?" Joe shuffled from foot to foot. "Well, I, um, I just help out."

The girls looked at each other and giggled some more.

"And d'you think you could help *me* out?" said Hi! Twin Two as her friend nudged her.

"Er, how?"

"Dance with the birthday girl?"

Joe glanced around the marquee, desperately looking for the girl whose eighteenth birthday party this was. When he and Matt had arrived and begun setting up earlier, the meal was still in full flow, with everyone holding up glasses of champagne to toast the very elegant-looking girl who wore a pink rose in her pinned-up hair.

"Where is she?" asked Joe, unable to locate her among the dancers and chatterers around the huge tent, and perplexed as to why the Hi! Twins wanted him to dance with her.

"Oi, dopey!" cackled Hi! Twin Two, her boozy breath washing over him. "'S me! *I'm* the birthday girl!"

Joe stared at her in confusion: the real birthday girl had looked effortlessly classy. This girl, along with her friend, was a bit of a mess. Quite attractive, yeah, Joe had to admit, but too wasted from the champagne to take seriously.

And then he saw the wilting pink rose that she'd shoved down her cleavage.

"Your hair..." he muttered.

"Oh, that," giggled Hi! Twin Two. "Too much like hard work. An' you know what they say – got to let your hair down!"

A torrent of giggles started up between the Hi! Twins and Joe looked at Matt pleadingly as the girls dragged him bodily on to the dance floor.

Matt just grinned and gave him the thumbs-up sign.

● ● ●

"And then she tried to–to—

"What?" laughed Matt, glancing round at Joe.

"Then..." Joe stared out at the beams of headlight that illuminated the pitch-black country road, his face contorted with disgust. "Then she tried to stick her tongue down my throat!"

Matt couldn't help sniggering. The one person in the world – or at least, in the marquee – who was least likely to respond to an enthusiastic, drunken snog was Joe. But Naomi – the real name of Hi! Twin Two – had been too tipsy to take that on board.

"Why are you laughing?" asked Joe. "I thought you'd be gutted, seeing as *I* got all the attention tonight, even though I didn't want it. That's more your scene, isn't it? Girls throwing themselves at you?"

"No worries, Joey," said Matt as the lights of the village appeared ahead. "I've got a nice little surprise for you."

"What?" asked Joe, worriedly, wondering what was coming next.

The street lamps of the village appeared on either side of the car as Matt drove along the main street towards the square.

"Naomi and Stella—"

"Who?" interrupted Joe.

"Naomi! The one with her tongue down your throat? And her mate? Remember?" Matt prompted, laughing again.

"What about them?"

Joe had an uncomfortable, sinking feeling in the pit of his stomach. Whatever Matt was going to come out with, he was pretty sure he wasn't going to like it.

"Well, we're going out with them next Friday."

"Are you *mad*!" squawked Joe, remembering Naomi's boozy breath and dirty laughter all over again. "It took all my energy to get that girl off me tonight. What the hell would I want to go out with her for?"

"'Cause I quite fancy her mate Stella, that's why. And Naomi's pretty gorgeous too," said Matt, turning into the quiet square and heading towards the turn-off to Joe's dad's house.

"Maybe, when she's sober..." grumbled Joe.

"Come on, it'll be a laugh!" Matt jollied him along, knowing that Joe wasn't going to go along with this arrangement without a barrel-load of encouragement.

"You must be joking! Why would I—"

"Joe!"

"Nah, let me finish, Matt! Why would I—"

"Joe – look!" Matt interrupted again, nodding at the scene in front of them.

Joe followed his gaze towards the flashing blue light of the ambulance that was parked outside his father's house.

CHAPTER 11

●●●●●●●●●●●●●●●●●●●●●●●●●●●●

A FEW HOME TRUTHS

Joe stared at the phone and willed it to ring.

He'd been doing that for the last two hours, as the light outside the kitchen window had turned from the darkness of the early hours of morning to the bright light of dawn. At first, Matt had hung around aimlessly, saying nothing helpful, until Joe finally told him to go and leave him alone.

"Miscarriage," his father had mumbled as he slid into the seat of his car and made to follow the speeding ambulance.

"Nothing," his father had snapped as Joe asked what he could do, holding on to the open car door.

"No!" he'd barked, slamming the door shut,

as Joe offered to come with him to the hospital.

Joe had stood frozen on the pavement, oblivious to Matt hovering by his side. For four years, the only tone Joe's father had used when he spoke to his son was apologetic. Simpering even. Tonight, there just seemed to be anger.

As the car pulled away, Robert Gladwin had rolled down the window and called in a less brusque voice: "Wait by the phone!" And, like the good son he was somewhere deep inside, Joe found himself waiting. And wondering. His head thumped with racing thoughts. All of them guilty.

He thought of the slow-motion moment when he'd leapt out of Matt's car, stared panic-stricken into the back of the ambulance, and felt that treacherous wave of relief when he'd seen that it was Gillian lying in there and not his father. He thought of how he'd spoken (or not spoken) to his father the day before, and how his dad must have been trying to tell him the news – the desperation to get him to come this weekend, the 'special' meal they were supposed to have – all scuppered by Joe's bad case of attitude.

He thought of Gillian's smile when he was trying to hide the camera he was borrowing for Maya, and how it didn't mask the fact that Gillian knew what he was doing but she was too nice to question him about it.

He saw again the quilted blanket in the wardrobe – Gillian had been collecting things for the baby. And he'd just thought she was childish.

Mad images skimmed across his brain of screaming babies. Some whining little brat who'd have been cooed over by Gillian and spoilt by his dad who, in his New Father role, would suddenly become a whole lot more interested in the parenting business than he had been the first time round.

Maybe it's right that this baby never happened, thought Joe in a crazy split second. *Maybe I'm glad.*

Joe shuddered as this terrible notion forced its way into his consciousness again and knew it wasn't true. Much as he resented – had spent *years* resenting – this cosy coupledom of Gillian and his dad, there was no way he'd wish anything this horrible on them.

But then maybe I'm to blame... he agonised, staring blankly at the silent phone.

The key rattling in the lock made him sit bolt upright and sent his pulse racing. His father's footsteps sounded heavy as he approached the kitchen.

"All right, Joe?" he nodded, standing in the doorway, eyes red-rimmed, looking tired and suddenly much older.

"Me?" Joe practically squeaked in surprise, the muscles in his throat constricted with tension. "Who cares about me? What about you? What about... Gillian?"

His father shrugged and gave a rumbling sigh that sounded like it was halfway towards being a sob. Joe felt as though he should be doing something vaguely useful – making strong tea or fixing his dad (or himself) a stiff drink. For a moment he even considered crossing the room and hugging his father – but that crushing guilt kept him pinned to his seat.

"She's– she's OK," said his dad, peeling off his jacket and throwing it over the back of a chair. He pulled the seat out and slumped down on it. "They're going to keep her in for a bit, just to be on the safe side."

"But the– the baby..." said Joe, clutching at straws, hoping that somehow the medical experts at the hospital had miraculously made everything all right. That was in spite of the evidence he'd seen for himself – the sight he'd glimpsed through his father's bedroom door of the bloody sheets on the bed. That terrible vision had been the reason he'd bellowed at a perplexed Matt to leave.

"No," his father said simply, shaking his head and staring at the patterned tablecloth that Gillian had spread out for their rushed meal the night before. "Listen, I think I'm going to get a couple of hours sleep, OK?"

"OK," muttered Joe, feeling completely out of his depth.

• • •

A few hours later, Robert Gladwin walked into a kitchen that smelt of fried breakfast and toast. He glanced at the newly bought Sunday newspapers on the table and then at his son.

"Been up the shop for some stuff. Started making you some breakfast." Joe looked shyly at his dad as he pulled plates out of the cupboard.

"Thanks, Joe," said his father, pulling out a chair. He looked over Joe's shoulder at the clock on the wall. "I'll just have some coffee for now. I've got to phone the hospital shortly and see how Gillian's doing. I hope I can bring her home today."

"Dad, I..." Joe began.

"Yes?"

"How old– I mean, how many months?" his son spluttered awkwardly.

"Nearly five months..."

Joe stopped.

Nearly five months? That was pretty far down the line. Why didn't I spot her... Gillian's bump yesterday? he asked himself, before realising why. Often enough, he'd thought cruelly of her as the pudgy Cabbage Patch Doll: he probably – ignorantly – assumed she was just getting fatter.

That's if I'd bothered paying her any attention at all.

"Nearly five months?" he said aloud. "Why did you wait this long to tell me?"

"Well, I wanted to," his dad began, rising up from his seat and opening a drawer in the pine kitchen dresser, "but I didn't want to do it over the phone. And you kept making excuses not to come and see us."

Joe felt like he'd been punched in the stomach. But worse was to come.

"Then, after we got this done," his dad continued, holding out a strange, blurry little black and white picture, "I really started to put pressure on your mum to get you out here. I thought we could have a nice meal... we could show you this... hope you'd be OK with the news... you know?"

"Did Mum know about the baby?" asked Joe quietly, not lifting his eyes from the hazy grey image of the scan he held in his hand.

"No – I wanted to tell you first. And... well, call me a coward, but I wanted to ask your advice on how to break the news to her."

The outline of the baby in the picture became fuzzier as hot tears of guilt prickled in Joe's eyes. His dad had hoped to speak to him like an adult, man to man, and Joe had acted like a sulky, bad-tempered kid, ruining their happiness and perhaps worse...

"It's my fault," muttered Joe, dropping his chin on to his chest.

"What? What's your fault?"

Joe glanced up at his father's confused face, and angrily wiped away the childish tears that were spilling down his cheeks.

"Losing the baby!" he spat the words out, disgusted with himself and his selfish behaviour. "If I hadn't spoilt everything, if I hadn't gone off last night, if I hadn't wound you guys up by—"

"Whoa, Joe!" Joe's dad interrupted him, holding his hands palm upwards. "Gillian losing the baby – it's got nothing to do with you!"

"But I acted like a total moron! I mean, she must have– I should have—" Joe struggled to get his thoughts in shape, running over the way he'd rushed through his food the night before, directing his few gruff snatches of small talk towards his dad and totally blanking Gillian, before rushing out of the door at the sound of Matt's car horn.

"I should have been nicer."

"Joey! Honestly, this has nothing to do with you or anything that has or hasn't gone on this weekend!" said his father agitatedly. "Miscarriages are one of those terrible, inexplicable things that sometimes just happen..."

Joe shook his head, too steeped in guilt to allow himself to believe his father. All he could see in front of him was the little alphabet quilt he'd come across in the wardrobe; the one that wouldn't be wrapped round a new baby.

"But—"

"But nothing! Gillian hadn't been feeling great for the past week, so this really, *really* isn't your fault, OK?"

The two of them stared wordlessly across the table at each other. It had been a long time since Joe had looked at his father with anything other than contempt in his eyes.

"OK?" repeated Robert Gladwin.

"Uh... OK," said Joe, finally giving in to his dad's reassurances.

He felt the warmth of his dad's fingers as they patted his hand and realised with a shock that it was probably the first time he'd had any physical contact whatsoever with his father since before the separation bombshell.

"God, Joe – I can't believe you've been sitting

here all this time blaming yourself!" his dad sighed and then smiled wryly. "Still, it makes a change from me feeling to blame for everything when it comes to you and your mum!"

"Huh?" said Joe, feeling weakened and disorientated after the emotional turmoil of the last few hours.

"I couldn't help it, you know, Joe," he smiled sadly. "It wasn't as though I went out looking for some seedy affair: I fell in love and there was nothing I could do about it. You don't choose when you fall in love – who with, or how right or wrong that is. You'll realise that yourself one day when it happens to you."

In the midst of his muddled feelings, Joe thought of a tumble of reddish curls, a smile so sweet and natural that it made Kerry's freckle-covered nose crinkle cutely... especially when Ollie made her laugh. Immediately, Joe felt a wave of understanding wash over him. Whatever the rights and wrongs of the original break-up, his father – whose only crime was to love someone – had had to carry the weight of his 'wrong-doing' with him every day, ever since.

And maybe that's a bit much to ask of anyone, Joe mused, wondering if maybe the time had come to ease up on his dad.

"You see, nothing's black and white, Joey," his

father smiled at him sadly. "Not even what happened with your mum and me."

"What do you mean?" asked Joe with a jolt.

"Well, it's not as if your mother's got a squeaky-clean past record when it comes down to it," his dad shrugged.

Instantly, Joe's warm feeling of reconciliation towards his father turned to ice in his veins.

CHAPTER 12

•••••••••••••••••••••••••••••

THAT'S WHAT FRIENDS ARE FOR

"Sonja?"

Anna hovered over her, carrying a pot of tea and two scones destined for the old ladies swapping gossip and tales of ailments at the small table by the jukebox.

"What's up?" Sonja grinned at the waitress.

"It's your mate, Joe," said Anna, nodding towards the rear of the café. "He's in the kitchen, up to his armpits in washing up."

"Oh, yeah, I forgot. He started working here today, didn't he?" said Sonja.

"Yeah, well, there's a lot sharp knives in that basin of water and he's looking so miserable, I'm scared he might find an alternative use for them, if you see what I mean."

"Really? What's wrong with him?"

"I don't know," shrugged Anna. "And I don't really know him well enough to ask. You don't fancy nipping through and having a word, do you?"

"Of course," said Sonja, hurriedly standing up. "Is it OK just to go through? I know Nick's not wild about people wandering through the back."

"It's fine. He's not due back for a bit and we'll be dead quiet out here for a while now the lunchtime rush is over."

"OK," nodded Sonja, scooping up the magazine she'd been about to flick through while she waited for some of the others to arrive. "Oh, Anna – Catrina and Matt are meant to be meeting me here. Give us a shout if they come in, will you?"

"No problem," Anna smiled as she glided her way over to the impatiently tutting old dears.

Rather than wending her way around the counter and past the old cappuccino machine that had a habit of spluttering out hot steam at unexpected moments, Sonja took the other route to the kitchen, pushing open the 'Staff Only' door in the short corridor that led to the loos.

"Hey, Joe!" she said cheerily to the stooped back and hunched-up shoulders in front of her.

"Hi," said Joe flatly, giving her a cursory glance over his shoulder.

"How's your first day going?" Sonja asked, keeping up the bright tone in her voice as she strode over and parked her bum against the draining board. There was no way Joe could avoid her now.

"All right," he answered, staring steadfastly at the bubble-filled sink and the pot he was scrubbing.

"And the weekend? How was it at your dad's?"

Joe said nothing, but stopped mid-scrub.

"Listen," said Sonja, more quietly now, "I spoke to Matt on the phone this morning – he told me about your dad's girlfriend losing her baby and everything..."

Joe lifted and dropped his shoulders miserably.

"That must have been awful, but at least you were there for your dad."

Sonja noted Joe's lack of reaction – she obviously hadn't hit the right button.

"And it must be weird for you, thinking you nearly had a baby brother or sister..."

Joe shuffled and Sonja knew from that tiny reaction that she'd said enough; it was down to Joe now.

"Yeah, that's done my head in a bit..." he finally responded, without making eye contact. "But it's more than just the– the baby."

"What? What's up, Joey?" she asked patiently.

Like Maya, she knew that Joe needed a bit of gentle coaxing to get his innermost feelings out in the open.

"I don't really want to talk about it," he said, giving Sonja an apologetic look.

"What about Ollie? Have you spoken to him about... whatever?" she asked, knowing that the bond between the boys ran deep.

"Nah," Joe shook his head. "I think he's a bit wrapped up in stuff at the moment."

"Stuff?" said Sonja, stumped for a second. "Oh, I get it. Stuff like Kerry, I suppose?"

"Yep," nodded Joe with the hint of an ironic smile on his face. "He finished his shift a while ago and went into town to buy her a one month and three days' anniversary present or something."

Sonja laughed. If Joe could make a joke, then it couldn't be all bad.

Still, pity his best mate can't see how Joe's feeling, she thought with irritation.

"Well, *I'm* not deserting you, Joe. *I'll* listen," said Sonja, sliding along the edge of the draining board and bumping him cheekily with her hip.

"Nah," smiled Joe ruefully. "I won't, if you don't mind."

"Please yourself," grinned Sonja, scooping up a handful of soapy bubbles and daubing them on his nose.

● ● ●

When Nick returned, Joe got ready to leave by the back door. He didn't fancy going through the café itself in case Sonja and the others were still there, among the gaggle of childminders and babies who'd congregated for afternoon tea and wailing. Sonja, full of good intentions, would be all set to push for a full confession. Again.

"Thanks for today, Joe. Same time tomorrow?" said Nick, tying on his white apron.

"Yeah, sure," nodded Joe, pushing open the heavy door.

Stepping out into the tiny back yard, he was greeted by three familiar faces. Sonja, Cat and Matt were all perched on old milk crates, and obviously waiting for him.

"Surprise!" shrilled Cat inappropriately.

"You didn't think you'd get away with mumfing about on your own, did you?" grinned Sonja as Matt shrugged sheepishly by her side.

● ● ●

Joe allowed them to lead him down to one of their favourite spots by the river. Far from being pressurised into talking about the weekend, he now sat listening to Catrina and Matt comparing notes on their problematic families.

"No way. Uh-uh." Catrina shook her head at Matt. "My situation's *much* worse than yours."

"Are you kidding?" said Matt heatedly, rising to the bait. "My mother is so wrapped up in her pink'n'fluffy pretty little daughters and her perfect new life that she can't be bothered with her angst-ridden, acne-covered teenage son."

"When have you ever been troubled with acne, Mr Perfect?" interrupted Sonja, squinting against the late afternoon sun as she stared at Matt's practically male-model-style handsomeness.

"Before I knew you lot," he answered defensively. "I wasn't *always* this gorgeous, y'know."

"Oooh!" gasped Cat at his mock arrogance and chucked a handful of grass at him.

Spitting out the blades of grass that landed on his teeth and lips, Matt tried to continue with what he was saying.

"I mean, even before she left, she and dad chose to make me a boarder at a school that was just down the road! How would any of you feel if your parents did that? And you can bet my precious half-sisters aren't going to be bundled off to some poxy boarding school..."

Joe nodded as he carried on chucking tiny pebbles into the river. He knew this was all for his benefit. They were trying to make him feel better about his own broken home.

"Yeah, fair enough," Cat conceded. "But at least you and Joe know *where* your runaway parents ended up. I wouldn't know how to find my dad – he could be living it up in Rio or down and out in London for all I know. He could be bigamously married to his fourth wife and have enough new kids to make a football team. Or he could be dead."

Joe shuddered at her last morbid – but feasible – point. It did put his own situation, unpleasant as it was, into perspective.

"OK, OK," he gave in. "I know you all want to know what's happened."

"Yeah, but not 'cause we want to get the gossip or sell your story to the papers," said Sonja, pushing herself up from her reclining position on the grassy river bank. "We just want to know 'cause we care about you and you've just been through a really freaky experience."

"I know," sighed Joe. Keeping what his father had told him to himself was giving him a skull-crushing headache. "Well, with what happened... It got me and my dad talking about stuff. Like why he left us and everything."

"That's good, isn't it?" asked Sonja hopefully.

"Kind of. But then he said something about

my mum. He said..." Joe took a deep breath. "He said he wasn't the only one who'd gone off with someone. He said that she had been fooling about with someone too."

"Your *mum*?" squealed Cat in disbelief. "But your mum's like a – a Sunday school teacher, she's so goody-goody! The word 'mumsy' was invented for your mum! She's got as much chance of having an affair as Snow White. She's—"

"And you've got as much chance of being tactful as I have of going out on a date with Michael Owen tonight!" snapped Sonja, attempting some damage limitation on her cousin's careless mouth.

"Did he tell you who with? Or when?" asked Matt.

"Not exactly," Joe shrugged, although he didn't feel exactly casual about the whole affair – he'd hardly slept for running it over and over in his mind. His own put-upon, badly treated mother acting the same way as his dad? He couldn't take it in.

"He said I'd have to ask her, if I wanted to know more."

"And did you?"

Joe looked at Sonja, and at his other two friends, and felt a certain amount of comfort at their concern.

"Nope," he shook his head. "I couldn't."

"God, Matt," said Catrina, staring at him with a beseeching gaze and reaching across the grass to pat his hand. "Brings it all back, doesn't it?"

For a second, as he watched his normally feuding friends' eyes lock together, Joe wasn't sure if Catrina was talking about family traumas or something else altogether...

CHAPTER 13

. . . .

SMILE, PLEASE!

"This is *fun!*"

"Ravi, get down from there," Maya chastised her brother gently, pulling his outstretched arm away from the mad-eyed bull and its alarmingly huge horns.

"Hey, Maya, let me take him off your hands for a while. You haven't managed to get any pictures yet, have you?"

Maya smiled at Brigid's niece gratefully.

"Thanks, Ashleigh," she smiled and rummaged in her pocket for her purse. "Here's some money for an ice cream for him..."

"Yeah and I'll take him over to the bouncy castle too, so take your time. Just meet us there when you're finished."

The bouncy castle lay at the far end of the

grounds set aside for the agricultural show, but the yells of bouncing children could be heard clearly over the noise of steam organs, mechanical machinery and mooing.

Breathing a sigh of relief at the prospect of some freedom, Maya turned and glanced around the crowded country park and wondered where to start.

When everyone from the photography club had gathered at the minibus earlier in the afternoon, Alex had been keen to point out to everyone the potential of the agricultural show.

"I know it sounds stuffy, but think about it," he'd said as a few dissenting groans had broken out when he'd told them where they were headed for their field trip. "Yes, so it's not glamorous, but an amazing amount of different people go to these shows and you could end up with some brilliant portraits for the competition."

"Will they accept a photo of a sheep then?" a boy whose name Maya couldn't remember had piped up from the back of the bus.

"Nothing in the rules to say they wouldn't," Alex had joked back. "But apart from farm animals, think about taking pictures of some of the characters who'll be there: crusty old farmers, prim old dears selling homemade jam, little brothers even!"

He shot an amiable glance at Maya, who'd been forced to take Ravi along with her for want of a better idea of what to do with him all afternoon.

"Oh, Ravi," she sighed under her breath as she set off towards a sea of large canvas tents to her left where a flower and vegetable show was advertised.

After her friends had beaten the guilt out of her on Saturday night at Sonja's sleepover, it had come back with a vengeance now that she'd dragged her little brother into the frame. Now *he'd* have to lie as well.

"Ravi, you understand, don't you?" she'd spelt out to him on the minibus earlier. "You can't tell anyone about this, OK? Not Mum and Dad, not Sunny, not your friends – all right?"

"What about Brigid? Can I tell her?" he asked, staring up with his serious big eyes.

"No, not even Brigid," Maya had said firmly. She knew Brigid would keep Maya's secret – especially since she'd put the idea of the club in her head in the first place – but didn't want to get her easygoing friend into any trouble, should her parents ever find out.

Ask first, ask first, she reminded herself of Alex's advice for snapping potential subjects as she strolled around.

The Konica that Joe had lent her the day before (he said his dad never used it and was happy for her to borrow it for a while) felt reassuringly heavy and professional in her hands. She'd spent some time in her room that morning, familiarising herself with the light meter and focus. Now all she had to do was find someone's photo to take.

She had no high hopes for the roll of snaps she'd eventually rattled off at Sonja's on Saturday on her rotten old camera, and didn't expect any miracles when she got a chance to develop them later on (once Ravi was safely dropped off back at home) in the clubhouse darkroom.

Time's running out, she acknowledged to herself, scanning the crowds for potential portraits. *I've got to get something today!*

On the approach to the tents, she saw them: two tweedy old farmers leaning up against a metal fence, staring at some rare breed of pigs the way Ollie drooled over manuals about vintage Vespas.

"Excuse me," she interrupted the men from their reverie. "I'm doing a project for a photography club. Would you mind if I took your picture?"

The men regarded her as if she was some exceptionally rare breed of alien – with surprise, distrust and awkwardness. It took a second for her to work out why. Except for the odd moron at school both in the city and in Winstead, she was always just Maya to anyone who came across her. To these grumpy old men, a young, pretty girl talking to them was bizarre enough; a young, pretty Asian girl was something they just didn't know how to deal with.

"Maya? Can I show you something?" a voice cut through the strained silence.

Maya flipped round to see Billy at her side.

"Sure, Billy," she nodded enthusiastically, desperate to get away from these strangely staring men. She followed as Billy led her off towards an old-fashioned pitch-your-strength fairground machine.

"Sorry to drag you away, but that didn't look much fun," he smiled at her, his piercing blue eyes gazing into hers. "And anyway, I need a hand..."

Maya watched as he quickly clambered up a metal railing and balanced precariously on the second-to-top bar.

"Can you just stand in front of me, so I can lean on you? I want to take a photo of this guy trying to hammer that machine..." he pointed at the colourfully painted pitch-your-strength "...and I think this angle would be more interesting."

"Sure," Maya agreed, already feeling his shins leaning into her back. It felt strangely nice, even though his knee was sticking uncomfortably into her neck.

"Maya?" Billy said from his elevated position, after a few clicks of the shutter.

"Yes?" said Maya, carefully moving her head up to look at him, so as not to disturb his balance.

Smiling down at her, Billy hit her with a question which surprised her so much that she nearly toppled him backwards into the neighbouring sheep pen.

"Could we maybe go out together sometime?"

CHAPTER 14

● ●

OH NO YOU DON'T!

Old school reports from primary school... a copy of a fading newspaper that featured a photo of Sunny in a school play, aged six... a pack of coloured felt pens that must have long since dried up... an old identity tag that belonged to Tia, the cat before Marcus...

"What are you doing?"

Maya thumped shut the lid of the wicker basket at the bottom of the hall cupboard at the sudden sound of her sister's voice.

"Just going through some old stuff," she said vaguely. Maya had been looking again for her school photography pictures, with no luck.

"What sort of stuff?" Sunny persisted, her arms folded defiantly across her chest as if she was some hotshot, Ally McBeal-type interrogator.

"Nothing much," Maya answered her dryly, rising up and closing the cupboard door. "Now, if you'll excuse me, I've got to get ready. I'm going out."

"Where are you going?" asked Sunny, following her sister up the stairs.

"My room," said Maya, hoping a small dose of sarcasm might get Sunny off her back.

"Not *now*, I mean where are you going *tonight*?" said Sunny, trailing after Maya into her room and flopping on to the bed.

"Out with Sonja and everyone. Just the usual Friday night," she shrugged.

Maya had a little rule about lying: repeat the lie as seldom as possible, so it didn't feel like such a bad thing to do.

"Yeah, but *where*?" asked Sunny, languidly banging one trainer-clad foot against the bed.

"Just the End for a while and then to the cinema," said Maya, mentally kicking herself: she'd already spun her parents the going-to-the-movies story and now here she was, letting the lie be spoken out loud again.

"What film are you going to see?"

"I don't know yet," answered Maya through gritted teeth as she pulled clothes out of the wardrobe.

"And is that the dress you're going to wear?"

"Yes," said Maya, unhooking the straps of her plum-coloured sheath dress from the hanger.

"Bit fancy just for going to the pictures, isn't it?" said Detective Sunny, lying sprawled on the bed, gazing at her big sister as if she could read her mind.

"Aaaark!"

Before Sunny could continue her line of questioning, she was interrupted by Marcus jumping lithely up on to Maya's bed.

"Hello, baby!" Sunny cooed, scratching the cat's head.

Undoing the buttons of her shirt to get changed, it struck Maya how much alike Sunny and Marcus were – skinny, long-legged, with big, brown, almond eyes that were full of mischief. They were both unashamedly nosy and had a talent for getting what they wanted.

But at least Marcus is cute and loveable, thought Maya, remembering all the occasions when Marcus curled his way affectionately around her legs. There was nothing cute and loveable about Sunny.

Maya slipped the dress over her head, pulled off her jeans and stepped into some flat, strappy black sandals. She'd fix up her hair and make-up later, in the loos at the café where she was meeting the others for their girly night out – no need to get Sunny started with any more "Why are you making such an effort?" comments now that she was distracted by playing with Marcus on the bed.

She nearly made it.

"What's in the bag?" quipped Sunny as Maya grabbed a little lace cardi and hauled her big black hessian saddlebag on to her shoulder.

"Nothing," Maya found herself lying again, slamming her bedroom door behind her as she left.

• • •

"Jeez, what have you got in here – a brick?" moaned Cat as she held Maya's bag.

"No," said Maya, looking up from a crouching position as she adjusted the strap on her sandal. "It's my new camera – well, Joe's camera."

"Aw, you shouldn't have bothered bringing that with you tonight! How can you dance lugging that thing around?" said Sonja disappointedly. As Entertainments Organiser for the evening, she wanted everyone to have fun – and if Maya had brought her camera and planned to take photos for this competition of hers, it could really put a damper on the night.

"But I just thought, y'know, girls out on the

town, all dressed up – it could be perfect for my project..." Maya answered apologetically. She stood up and took her bag from Cat as the three girls continued walking along the high street.

"Girls out on the town? Huh! Make that *some* girls out on the town..." Cat snorted, the diamanté clasps in her hair glinting as she tossed back her blonde curls.

"Oh, don't start that again!" snapped Sonja. She was as annoyed with Kerry as Cat was, and suspected – like her – that Kerry hadn't so much dropped out of this evening because of a cold as she'd told them, but because she wanted to spent a cosy night in with Ollie instead. That said, it wasn't worth ruining the night moaning on about her absence: they could have fun enough without her, Sonja had reasoned.

"Didn't you get enough pictures last weekend?" Cat asked Maya, giving Sonja a don't-snap-at-me haughty look.

"They didn't come out so great – I was still using my old camera, so the quality was pretty crummy once I got them developed."

"What about that thing you went to at the country park on Wednesday? Didn't you get anything good there?" Sonja chipped in.

"I haven't developed them yet," Maya answered, switching the bag to her other shoulder. There was one thing to be said for her cheap'n'nasty little snapper – the pictures weren't much cop, but it sure weighed a lot less than the Konica. "And I just don't know if I got my shot that day."

"Well, how could you, since you had your mind on *other* matters?" Cat teased.

"I– I– didn't..." Maya faffed, feeling a blush rise to her cheeks. She'd tried to be as casual as she could when Billy had asked her out, saying "Sure", as if going out on a date was something she did all the time. But Cat was right – it had blown her concentration for the rest of the day. The rest of the week, in fact.

"Oh, good – not too much of a queue," Sonja interrupted as they turned off the high street and headed down towards the bus station – and the Enigma nightclub.

Now, instead of her heart pounding about her impending date, Maya's heart began to race at the idea of walking into a club. Suddenly, she felt it must be blindingly obvious that she was just sixteen; as if she had her age tattooed on her forehead for all the world – and the bouncers of Enigma – to see.

"Don't worry," smiled Sonja, knowing instinctively what was going through Maya's mind. "Girls never have any hassle getting in."

Maya nodded as they joined the short queue and tried to feel reassured. But sneaking in under-age to a club wasn't something that made her feel comfortable, even if Cat and Sonja made it sound so easy. And the knowledge of how outraged her parents would be if they knew didn't make her feel too good either.

"Anyway, stuff boys, stuff parents, stuff Kerry for being a party-pooper – let's just have a night to remember!"

Maya laughed at Cat's enthusiastic outburst and tried to relax. If Cat and Sonja weren't worried, then neither was she.

"Yes, love, go on through... Sorry, lad, no trainers... Go through... Yes, straight through, love..." The doormen on either side of the entrance ushered the waiting punters through.

"Fine, straight through..." said the doorman nearest the girls, waving Catrina in.

"And you too, nice and quick, thanks..." he nodded at Sonja.

"Hold on, love, I'll need to check your bag," said the other doorman as an arm came out in front of Maya, stopping her in her tracks.

"Move ladies. No blocking the door, please!" a male voice boomed. Maya glanced up to see Sonja and Cat being motioned forward and heard Sonja yell, "Meet you inside!"

Feeling beads of sweat forming on her forehead, Maya folded her slightly shaking hands across her chest as the besuited giant rummaged in her bag.

It's OK, she reassured herself, aware of two bored-looking disco dollies in nearly matching pink dresses snickering at her predicament. *This is just a security check – it's got nothing to do with my age.*

"Thanks, love," growled the doorman as he handed back the saddlebag.

Relieved, Maya took it from him – but found he hadn't let it go.

"Er, how old are you, love?"

Maya looked up at the two-metre high, metre-wide human doorstop and suddenly felt very small and fragile.

"Eighteen..." she whispered unconvincingly.

"Got any proof of that, love?"

"Er, no. I don't think I brought anything out with me tonight..."

"Then sorry, no can do."

"But my friends..." she protested feebly, pointing towards the entrance to the club.

The doorman wordlessly shook his head at her.

What was it that my horoscope said on Saturday? thought Maya, thinking back to Sonja's sleepover as she turned and trudged miserably up towards the high street, tears of disappointment and embarrassment stinging her eyes. *'A night out with friends will be full of surprises.'* Well, that sounds about right...

CHAPTER 15

● ●

"HI!"S AND LOWS

"Look – isn't that Cat and Sonja running along the road?"

"Uh, yeah, looks like it," Matt agreed with Joe, scrunching up his eyes to focus all the better on the distant, receding figures. "And it looks like they're trying to catch up with Maya."

"Wonder what they're up to then?" said Joe balefully, wishing he was spending the evening hanging about with the girls instead of going on this double date Matt had set up.

In fact, he'd tried hard to wriggle out of it. After the trauma of the last week he wasn't exactly in the mood for partying, but Matt wouldn't take no for an answer. Had even told Joe it would do him good.

"Don't know," shrugged Matt as they

approached the turning that led down to Enigma. "They were on a girls' night out tonight, weren't they? They didn't say what they had planned."

"Well, at least they're not going to Enigma," said Joe with a certain amount of relief. He couldn't have handled Kerry seeing him getting flustered and tongue-tied as he tried to talk to some stupid girl he hardly knew.

At the thought of Kerry, he squinted ahead, but couldn't see any of the girls now – traffic from the junction obscured his view.

"That's a good point. We don't need them messing up our chances with Naomi and Stella by cackling away at us."

Joe threw a quick look at his friend. Matt was obviously anticipating some kind of action tonight and the thought of it made Joe's heart start hammering in panic. Yes, he had girl *friends*, but he'd never had an actual girlfriend. Or been out on a date for that matter.

How can I match up to Matt and all his experience? thought Joe as they turned a corner and the Enigma nightclub came into view.

Standing close to the entrance to the club, two girls in spookily similar sugar-pink minidresses began waving at them.

"Brilliant – they're here already," smirked Matt, giving the girls a half-hearted, casually cool wave back. "By the way, I told them that you're an unemployed musician."

"What?" Joe burst out. "Why did you do that?"

"Because Naomi's eighteen and at college. You've a much better chance of getting a snog if she thinks you're a bit more interesting than a seventeen-year-old schoolboy," said Matt with a grin. "But if she's not interested in you, then Stella isn't going to be interested in me. Geddit?"

"Oh, great! So for the sake of your love-life, I've got to pretend I'm an eighteen-year-old drummer on the dole, then?"

"Nah..." Matt shook his head. "I said you were nineteen."

"Gee, thanks!" hissed Joe as they came within a few feet of the Hi! Twins. "And did it slip your mind to tell me or did you just leave it till now in case I flipped out and said I wouldn't come?"

"Something like that," Matt hissed back with a knowing smile. "Hi there, girls!"

"Hi!" trilled Naomi and Stella in unison.

● ● ●

"You..." said Naomi, ramming her finger repeatedly in Joe's chest. Her piercing blue eyes seemed to be struggling to get him into focus.

Joe waited a while, wondering what she was going to say next. Even in the darkened club he could see how flushed her cheeks were as a result of too many vodka and Cokes.

"What?" he asked finally as her sentence trailed off. The jabbing finger was still working though.

"You... you are *weird*."

"Am I?"

"Yep."

"Why?"

"Because... because..."

Because I've kept my hands to myself and haven't tried to snog your face off yet, Joe finished her sentence inwardly.

He didn't feel he could handle this for much longer; his brain was too frazzled with bigger issues to deal with this ridiculous situation. Joe looked away from Naomi's drunkenly accusing expression to the dance floor, where Matt and Stella seemed to be doing their version of the lambada (with lips and hips in constant contact) to some slow and whiny Celine Dion track.

Just 'cause I believe you have to know and like a person reasonably well before you kiss them – if that makes me weird, then fine, Joe told himself, watching Matt's antics.

Just 'cause I don't happen to think a few drinks

*and a grope on a dance floor is romantic – fine.
Just 'cause—*

"Oi, you! I'm talking to you!"

The jabbing became more insistent. Joe looked back at Naomi and realised that, just as it had happened at her party, a transformation had come over her after she'd had a few drinks. When they'd met outside the club, she'd seemed quite pretty (not Joe's type – but then, only one girl was Joe's type) but now Naomi's soft, round features had turned into a boorish, boozy snarl.

Did I look like this when I was drinking? he wondered. Uncomfortable memories of his own alcohol-fuelled exploits flooded into his mind as he watched the girl in front of him make a fool of herself.

"Is there something wrong with you?" Naomi sneered.

"Like what?"

"Don't you *like* girls or something?"

"Yeah! Yeah, of course I do!" Joe stuttered, suddenly aware that Naomi was insinuating that he might be gay, just because he didn't happen to fancy her.

"But just not me?"

"No – it's not that. I just—"

"Think you're really something, don't you?"

"What?"

"You're an arrogant, big-headed pig!" she spat out with venom in her voice.

Joe stared at her in silence, completely stumped. She could have called him all sorts of things: shy, awkward, introverted, difficult even. But arrogant? Big-headed?

Before he could try and reason out her thinking any further, he found that Naomi had one more surprise for him.

CHAPTER 16

●●●●●●●●●●●●●●●●●●●●●●●●●●●

ACT NATURAL

"This spotty guy behind the counter just kept staring at us and *staring* at us..."

"Well, I don't suppose they often get girls glamming up to come and sit in Burger King for their Friday night out, do they?" Sonja interrupted as Cat relayed the events of that evening to the others.

"Oh, don't go telling lots of good stories while I'm too busy to stop!" Ollie moaned as he passed by, laden with plates covered in the remains of Sunday morning fry-ups.

"Don't worry, Ollie," Maya called after him, a wry smile on her face, "they're just having a laugh at my expense, that's all!"

"You poor thing!" said Kerry, imagining herself in the same position. She'd sneaked into a few strictly over-eighteen venues and had felt just as nervous as Maya. Luckily, she'd never been caught the way Maya had. Yet. "You must have been mortified!"

"Mmm," muttered Maya, raising her eyebrows. "It was just the fact that I didn't know what to do with myself – and wondering what the girls would be thinking, waiting inside for me."

"And we just stood in the corridor for a bit," Sonja took up the story, "then when there was no sign of Maya—"

"—I stuck my head out the door and asked one of the bouncers where she'd gone," Cat continued.

"I don't think I've ever been so glad to hear Cat's high heels clip-clopping behind me," Maya smiled across the Formica table.

"Oh and you looked like little orphan Annie, moping up the high street in your party frock with nowhere to go!" said Cat, sticking out her bottom lip for effect.

"And that's when we decided, sod it! Comfort eating, here we come!" Sonja continued, remembering how they'd dragged Maya into the fast food joint to spend the rest of the evening eating, commiserating and giggling.

"At least it's a small comfort to know you guys had a worse night than us!" Catrina snickered.

Matt hadn't been able to resist spilling the beans about their night out – especially the last part.

"Yeah, I still can't get over that! Some stupid cow slapping our Joey's face," said Sonja, throwing her arm protectively around him. "How could she?"

"He's all right about it, aren't you, Joey?" said Matt amiably. "We had a laugh about it on the way home, didn't we?"

"Did we?" Joe responded flatly. Although it had happened on Friday evening, he still felt slightly in shock after being at the wrong end of Naomi's drunken rage. And he was so relieved when Stella came rushing over after seeing what had happened and had dragged her sozzled mate off to get a taxi.

He'd spent yesterday avoiding everyone. He just couldn't bear the thought of them all giggling about it.

"Anyway, I don't know how *you* can laugh," Sonja said pointedly to Matt. "Considering you're no stranger to having a girl deck you one."

Cat broke out into a tuneless whistle, gazing at the ceiling, all innocence, with a smirk on her lips.

"Yeah, but that was a long time ago," said Matt straight-faced, in response to Sonja's dig about the time he and Catrina had gone out together for a while and then broken up – messily. "And it was only Cat's way of showing how much she cared about me!"

"Oooh, you!" gasped Cat, turning and thumping him on the arm, trying not to laugh at the same time.

"OK, OK, truce!" Maya cried out, before war was declared. "What's important is that I still didn't get my photo, so..." she dragged the chunky camera out of her bag "...I want your help!"

"What?" said Matt, pretending not to understand, but running his fingers through his hair and turning his face to profile. "Is there something we can do?"

"Yes," nodded Maya. "But you can quit those catalogue poses right now, Matt. I want you all to carry on talking while I wander round the table and take spontaneous pictures of you."

"How can they be spontaneous if you're telling us you're doing it?" asked Joe, panic-stricken at the idea.

"For me, Joe, please," pleaded Maya. "I'm running out of time for this portrait competition next weekend!"

Joe nodded while the others giggled and tried, with varying degrees of success and fooling around, to carry on with their conversations.

Twenty minutes later, Maya felt the shutter button resist as she pressed it and knew that she'd used up all her film.

"It's a wrap!" she smiled at her friends, sliding back on to the red leather banquette beside Matt.

"Well, thank you, Ms Spielberg! Now can we go? Some of us have other commitments!" joked Sonja, clambering over Joe to get out of the booth. Joe looked slightly flustered.

"Me too," nodded Cat as she stood up. "Me and Mum have been invited for Sunday lunch round Sonja's, so I better go and practise being a lovely daughter."

"Don't waste your time, Cat," said Sonja with a wicked grin. "You're not going to fool anyone in my family after all these years."

"I'll give you guys a lift round, if you want," Matt offered, scooping up his car keys from the table. "I've got to get back and catch my dad when he gets home from golf. I need my allowance before he shoots off to London later today."

"Aww, isn't that sweet," teased Cat, chucking him under the chin. "What a loving son you are!"

Joe watched the two of them and wondered again if there was anything brewing up once more between them. It would probably mean trouble, but who could stand in the way of love...?

"'Scuse, Joe!" said Kerry, following Sonja out

of the booth. "I promised to take Lewis to feed the ducks this afternoon."

Joe stood up and breathed in deeply as Kerry shuffled past. She always smelled of something light and sweet.

Like coconut, he thought as he felt the warmth of her slip past him.

"Just me and you then, Joe," he heard as the café door jangled shut.

"Yep," he said to Maya, who'd settled herself across the table from him.

"Listen, I heard about what went on at your dad's last weekend," Maya began. "Doesn't sound like a lot of fun."

"No," Joe acknowledged.

"Have you spoken to your mum yet about... what your dad said?"

"No," Joe answered, playing with the glass salt and pepper set on the table.

"Did you at least tell her about the baby?"

"Nope."

"You should, you know," Maya smiled sadly at him. "Take it from me, secrets make you miserable."

Joe stared across the table at his friend. He wanted to ask her all about her own worries, her own problems, but he was too shy to ask, unless she offered the information.

"We're kind of the same, aren't we, Joe?"

Joe stared at Maya, wondering how this beautiful, serious girl could consider herself anything like his bumbling self.

"The others – they all show their emotions up front, don't they?" she said rhetorically. "Me and you – we always try and sort it out ourselves, but sometimes it doesn't work, does it?"

She was right, Joe knew. The others, including Ollie when he wasn't wrapped up in love, always had to prise any information out of him. But their suggestions and advice always somehow made things more bearable.

"How are you feeling right now?" she asked him bluntly.

"What – apart from the total humiliation of having someone dislike me so much that they slap my face?"

"Mm-hm. Apart from that," nodded Maya with a little grin.

"Um, kind of like I've got this big weight on my shoulders."

"Me too," shrugged Maya. "But with me, I don't know how I can get free of the feeling. Right now, I can't see how I can make things better with my parents, how I could magically make them less strict."

Joe nodded. He knew a lot of Asian parents

were quite strict with and ambitious for their children; but then, so were plenty of other families. Part of him wanted to ask if it was a cultural thing in Maya's case, but part of him felt that was too embarrassing and gauche a question to ask.

"But at least *you* can try and resolve things," she continued. "At least if you talk to your mum – even if she tells you stuff that's hard to hear – it'll be better than keeping quiet and letting it wind you up inside."

"Yeah, I know you're right," said Joe. "I'll try and talk to her soon."

"And you should tell the others that you hate being called Joey. They probably don't even realise. But it really gets to you, doesn't it?"

Joe looked at her in astonishment. "Ever thought about being a psychologist?"

"I think that's on the potential career list my parents have drawn up for me, actually," said Maya, smiling back at him.

• • •

Maya was still thinking about her conversation with Joe when a thundering crash jolted her back to the real world. Stepping out of her bedroom, she saw a stepladder lying in the middle of the landing and her sister's head hanging upside down from the opened attic trapdoor.

"Oops!" said Sunny, her sleek one-length bob looking ridiculous hanging the wrong way up.

"What happened?" asked Maya, bending over to pick up the ladder. It crossed Maya's mind that it might be fun to leave her sister up there for a while, but Sunny could shriek just as annoyingly and loudly as Marcus, so that would get on her nerves pretty quickly.

"I was just trying to come down, but it wobbled when I stood on it..."

"Yes, but what are you doing up there in the first place?"

Maya started climbing the upturned ladder as she talked, curious to have a peek at the long-unopened attic.

"I was looking for some old clothes I could use for my play. Mummy said there were lots up here, stored away."

"Move over," Maya said to her sister as she clambered into the loft space.

Sunny bunched up the long dress she'd shoved on top of her normal clothes and shuffled over to make way.

"I'd forgotten about all this," said Maya, surveying the old trunks and cardboard boxes surrounding her. It suddenly occurred to her that this might be the place to look for her old photography project. "Come across any of my old school stuff while you were rummaging?"

"Maybe..." shrugged Sunny. "There were some exercise books and exam papers in among the old photos in that box over there."

Maya walked over to the box Sunny had indicated and sat down cross-legged beside it.

"Don't let me stop you doing what you were doing," she said, aware of Sunny's inquisitive gaze boring into the side of her head.

Sunny tutted and, knowing she was being told to leave, reluctantly slid through the trapdoor with much rustling of fabric.

Like the wicker basket in the hall cupboard, there was a real mishmash of old papers and memorabilia, plus a few pictures of her mother's parents – Grandpa Naseem and Nana Jean. And there was a whole album of photos of her father's family that Maya hadn't seen for years.

It was fascinating to flick through; unlike Grandpa Naseem and Nana Jean who came to visit regularly, she'd never met her paternal grandparents. They'd moved to Canada to live with her uncle and his family when she was a baby.

They looked stern in these pictures, which must have been at least twenty years old judging by the style of the furniture and the suit Grandpa Ravinder was wearing.

There's Dad, she found herself smiling fondly at the photo of her father as a student, standing beaming at the top of a mountain he'd just climbed with some friends. *Pity he doesn't look that relaxed and happy more often...*

She flipped through more pictures of a handsome, happy-go-lucky young man, who seemed a world away from her dad as she knew him today.

And there's him and Mum, she said to herself as her eye caught a slightly blurry picture she'd never paid much attention to before.

She gazed at the small photo of the young man, staring straight at the camera, and the besotted, pretty Indian girl who was gazing up at him. The boy, slimmer and happier looking, was still recognisably her dad. The girl, on closer inspection – was most definitely *not* her mother...

CHAPTER 17

●●●●●●●●●●●●●●●●●●●●●●●●●●●●

OPEN MOUTH, INSERT FOOT

Searching for her keys before she left for the photography club, Maya was only half-listening to the conversation that was going on in the kitchen.

"What are they? Balloons?" she heard Brigid ask.

"*No!*" said Ravi with a note of outrage in his voice. "It's a drawing of little piglets – seven of them!"

"Seven? My, my," Brigid's voice drifted though. "And what made you think of drawing seven little piglets, then?"

"They were at the fair I went to last week with Maya and those other people. We..." he trailed off, suddenly realising he'd told what he wasn't meant to tell.

"What fair was that, Ravi?"

"It was a secret. I wasn't meant to say... was I, Maya?"

Ravi stared up as his alarmed-looking sister appeared in the doorway of the kitchen.

"Ooh, look at the time, Ravi – *Blue Peter* will be on soon. Off you go and watch it," Brigid smiled at him, then looked up at Maya and motioned her to sit down at the kitchen table. "Now, since when did you take him to a fair?"

"Um, it was last Wednesday. It was that big agricultural show – the one at the country park," Maya answered, wriggling in her seat like a kid who had been caught ringing the neighbours' doorbells and then running away.

"And why is that a secret? Your mother and father wouldn't have a problem with you taking Ravi along to the likes of that!" Brigid's penetrating green eyes bore into Maya.

"No... but they'd have a problem if they knew I was there with that club I've joined."

"Ah, the photography club up at the Education Centre. Yes, my Ashleigh said she'd seen you there. And are you enjoying it?"

Maya was caught on the hop. She'd expected Brigid to give her some kind of lecture, but now here she was enquiring pleasantly about her new hobby.

"Y-yes... I think I'm going to love it,' Maya answered her cautiously. "Our lecturer has got us all entering a competition already – at the Peacock Gallery."

"Really? Well, that's nice," Brigid nodded. "I'm glad you decided to join the club and I'm glad you like it so much. I thought you would – that's why I tried to put the idea in your head in the first place. But..."

Ah, I haven't got out of it yet, winced Maya.

"I didn't mean for it to get you into more complications with your parents."

"Brigid, I—"

"Now, Maya, let me finish," interrupted Brigid. "We may not speak about it out loud, but me and you have an understanding, don't we?"

"Yes, I guess so," Maya muttered.

"I understand that, as a young adult, you need a bit more freedom than your parents are willing to give you. Is that right?"

Maya nodded, wilting under Brigid's stern gaze.

"And *you* understand that I'll keep quiet about you meeting up with your friends most days and doing something like this photography course, right?"

Maya nodded again.

"The thing is, Maya, you and me keeping

secrets, it's not ideal. Your folks are lovely people at heart – but the way I see it, it's not hurting them, and I know you're a good girl who isn't running around wild."

I wish they would think that way, Maya said to herself.

"Now, here's my problem: you're sixteen and responsible for your own actions. But you can't go involving a seven-year-old boy in a web of lies!"

"I didn't ask him to lie!" Maya protested, miserable at her confidante's disapproval. "I had to take Ravi with me on this field trip because I was babysitting him, and I thought it would be easier to tell him it was a secret, rather than risk him blabbing about me being part of this photography club!"

"Maya, you can't put pressure like that on a little lad! It's not right and it's not fair to involve him!"

What Brigid was saying was true, she knew, but Maya still didn't know what else she could have done.

"Y'know, I think you maybe should tell your folks about this club, rather than get deeper and deeper into a mess over it," Brigid continued.

"But it's only you and me that know about it! I'll just tell Ravi not to tell—"

"Maya, you did that before and he accidentally let it slip to me. He'll do it again – he's only a child."

"But if I tell them, they'll be furious – me doing something behind their backs. Something so frivolous... They'll stop me from going!"

"Ah now, maybe they will and maybe they won't," Brigid smiled at her kindly. "But I don't see what choice you really have after this. And anyway, what if you do well in this competition? Shows at that gallery are always in the local paper – what if your parents open the newspaper one day and there's your name plastered under some photo or other?"

"I *won't* win anything. I've only just started and there'll be hundreds of entries from all over!" Maya argued weakly.

"Well, it's up to you, Maya. All I'm saying is that all these secrets are maybe just getting a bit out of hand..."

"I know," said Maya forlornly, before suddenly spying the time. "Oh, Brigid, I've got to run – I've, er, got the photography club tonight and I've got so much to do to get my entry ready for the competition on Saturday."

"You will be back before your folks, though?"

"Um, no – I already told them I'd be out tonight."

Brigid furrowed her brow.

"And where exactly did you tell them you'd be?"

"Round at Sonja's for tea," said Maya grimacing, aware of another lie surfacing.

"Oh, Maya!" scolded Brigid.

Before her sister could leave the kitchen and catch her eavesdropping in the hallway, Sunita slipped quietly into the living room...

• • •

"Nice. Very nice. Yep, that's the one I'd go for."

Alex was peering at the contact sheets of tiny prints from Maya's last two rolls of film. As she'd suspected, her shots of passers-by and piglets from the country park show were nothing to write home about, but the photos she'd taken at the End on Sunday had come out pretty well.

"The composition's great in it and everyone looks relaxed and unaware of the camera. What do you think?"

Maya took the small magnifying glass from him and bent over the contact sheet to look at the shot Alex had circled.

There, in miniature, were her friends, all gathered round their favourite table at the End. As this was shot 34 of a 36-frame spool, by this point they'd managed to lose their self-consciousness and seemed almost to have forgotten, in the midst of their conversation and the noise and hubbub of the café, that Maya was hovering around snapping them.

She peered at the group: Matt and Catrina had their backs to her, but their faces were in profile as they stared each other down.

Probably trading insults as usual, thought Maya.

On the other side of the table, Kerry was waving. At first, Maya had assumed she was waving at her, but on closer inspection, her gaze was going past Maya's head, presumably towards Ollie, who was busily whipping around the café, seeing to the needs of the Sunday morning breakfasters.

Next to Kerry sat Sonja, her mouth wide in mid-chatter, and on Sonja's right was Joe, who looked more dazed than usual – as well he might with everything going on in his family life. Or maybe it was just that he was gazing in stunned wonder at Sonja's ability to yap without pausing for breath.

"Yes, you're right," Maya agreed with Alex. "I'll get this one printed up."

"Bit of a queue happening over there," Alex alerted her to the list of names as everyone vied for time in the darkroom. "Last minute panic and everything. Are you OK to stay a little longer tonight to get this done?"

"Yes, no problem," said Maya. As she'd told Brigid, her parents thought she was at Sonja's. And as she *hadn't* told Brigid, the other reason she'd be home later was that she had a date with Billy after the club.

Maya couldn't decide which was thumping harder – her heart through nerves, or her head from the stress of keeping secrets.

● ● ●

"Maya... That's a beautiful name. What does it mean?"

"Um, I don't know actually," Maya answered, racking her brain for a memory of her mother telling her anything more about her name, other than it belonging to some favourite auntie on one side of the family.

Billy smiled at her across the chequered tablecloth and looked ridiculously handsome.

Don't get flustered, Maya told herself. *He's just a boy, like Joe and Ollie and Matt, and I don't get all embarrassed when I talk to them.*

"You don't mind that we just came for a pizza, do you?" he asked before she could come up with any conversation herself. "I don't know about you, but I'm a bit skint – a fiver for a pizza was all I could afford. We could've gone for a burger, of course, but then that's not very..."

Romantic? Maya silently finished his sentence for him as she watched him blush slightly.

"No, it's fine, I love pizza and I've never been here before," she smiled encouragingly, gazing round the restaurant at the overblown but cosy Italian decor.

"Not what you're used to, though," he smiled back at her, looking a little more confident again.

Maya gave a half-laugh, wondering what on earth he meant.

Does he think I only go to fancy restaurants? Or that I never eat out at all? she puzzled to herself.

"I mean – and maybe I'm rushing a bit here – I'd love to go out to an Indian restaurant with you sometime," he beamed as if about to give her a big compliment. "You must know so much about all the amazing food – I always just have the same thing and go for a chicken tikka massala every time!"

"Well," said Maya, still trying to figure out where he was going with this, "if ever I go to an Indian restaurant, I always go for a vegetable korma. I don't really like hot food."

Billy laughed as if that was the funniest thing he'd heard in ages.

"But what about at home? What do you tend to have at home?"

"Whatever Brigid, our home help, makes for us," Maya answered, her fixed smile now fading fast.

"Ah, right..." It was Billy's turn to look confused. "So, uh, how long have you been here?"

"In this restaurant? About twenty minutes," she answered him straight-faced, using the same sarcastic tone of voice she usually kept for Sunny. Then, seeing his face drop, she softened it by adding: "I've lived in Winstead for about a year and a half now."

"And where were you born?" he continued clumsily.

"London. Where were you born?" Maya was starting to feel irritated.

"Me? Oh, I'm just a Winstead boy, born and bred. Very boring."

Too right, thought Maya. *What's he going to ask next – if he can see my sari collection?*

"Have you ever, you know, been back for a visit?"

"To London?" she asked, deliberately misunderstanding him.

"No," he laughed nervously, sensing her

irritation but not really taking it on board. "I mean India."

"No – my parents prefer skiing holidays," she answered flatly.

Maya could see what he was doing: trying to fit her into some stereotype without even getting to know her first. She could almost see herself through his eyes as some exotic Hindu princess with a deep, innate sense of the mystical world, a talent for making chapatis and a video cabinet full of Bollywood classics.

But I'm none of those things! she seethed inwardly. *I'm me, I'm British, I'm the same as all my friends. I like chart music, Ewan McGregor, watching Disney videos with my little brother, and strawberry sundaes the way Nick makes them down at the End. How dare he make assumptions about me?*

"They prefer skiing? Wow, that's amazing!" Billy said in astonishment.

You may be pretty, thought Maya, staring stony-faced at the tactless boy opposite her, *but you're also pretty stupid.*

CHAPTER 18

• •

DEEPER AND DEEPER

"Maya!" said Sonja in surprise. "I didn't expect to see you tonight!"

Maya lifted her eyebrows tellingly and slid into the booth beside Sonja and Kerry.

"I just thought I'd take a diversion on the way home, in case any of you were still here."

"Well, we are for the next ten minutes – until Nick throws us out," said Sonja looking pointlessly at the wonky clock on the wall that pointed to twelve. "So what happened to your date? Didn't exactly last very long, did it?"

"No. It wasn't a whole lot of fun so I bailed out early. Said I had a headache."

"Why? What happened?" asked Kerry with concern. She and Sonja had only just finished idly wondering how Maya was doing on her first date and keeping their fingers crossed for her. The last thing they expected was to see her wandering into the End at ten to nine.

"Why? How about he was a patronising git?" said Maya, relieved to be in good company after an hour's worth of tortuous conversation with Billy.

"In what way? Did he act like you were thick or something?" asked Sonja incredulously. No one she knew was smarter than Maya.

"No – he just had all these preconceptions about me; asking me things like how did I feel about arranged marriages and Buddhism and stuff..."

"God, that's a bit heavy for a first date, isn't it?" Sonja winced.

"I know! I couldn't believe it – like I'm the Indian cultural attaché to Winstead," said Maya, wrinkling her nose in disbelief. "I mean, what do I know? My parents aren't religious; they didn't have an arranged marriage – it's not like I'm an expert, is it?"

As Kerry shook her head in sympathy, Sonja took a long look at her friend.

"But Maya, why does it bug you so much that he asked you all those sort of questions?" she said pointedly. "I've had all that kind of thing too, you know. Just because my mum's Swedish, I get all the questions like I know the country inside out. And I've had a million boys doing fnar-fnar jokes about Swedish porn."

"Yes, but it's not the same – he was just making so many presumptions about me, about who I am and what I'm like."

"Everyone makes judgements about what people are like from the way they look," Sonja tried to reason. "Whether that's right or wrong or good or bad, it's just the way people are – trying to look for clues to someone's personality through the way they dress or the colour of their hair – whatever."

"That's true," nodded Kerry. "It's like Cat; because of the way she dresses and everything, people who don't know her tend to think she's a bit, well, *tarty*, when we all know..."

Kerry's argument fizzled out as she looked at the other girls' faces.

"OK, OK, maybe Cat wasn't a good example," she found herself laughing.

"Maya, do you hate being labelled because of what happened when you first arrived at St Mark's?" asked Sonja astutely, remembering the racial taunts that Maya had had to endure from a couple of moronic girls when she joined their school.

Cat, who'd been in two of Maya's classes, told

Sonja and Kerry about the new girl's problems and together they'd all had a quiet word with the bullies (Kerry standing at the back for moral support while the two girls got an earful from the forceful duo of Cat and Sonja). Out of sympathy, the three of them had adopted the friendless Maya at the same time, but quickly became as fond of and inseparable from her as she was from them.

"No!" said Maya vehemently. "It's just– I mean, he shouldn't have—"

"Listen, you should think about it, Maya," Sonja interrupted. "Sure, you're the same as us, but you do have another whole aspect to your life, courtesy of your family – we all do. And I just think it sounds like you're being a bit hard on this Billy guy. It's not like he insulted you or anything."

Maya didn't reply but just looked down at the table. Along with Brigid's, this made her second lecture of the day, and the second that she grudgingly had to accept made sense.

• • •

"Hi, I'm home!" shouted Maya, closing the door behind her and hanging her jacket up on the coat-rack.

"Hello?" she said, pushing the living room door open and wondering why no one had responded.

Three sets of eyes stared at her. Her father was sitting rigidly in his armchair. Her mother was perched poker-straight on a chair by the writing desk, with Marcus curled up but awake on her lap.

"Mum?" said Maya, slightly frightened by how silent they were.

"Did you have a nice time at Sonja's?" her mother asked finally.

"Um, yes…" Maya answered, still stranded in the doorway, reluctant to step any further into the atmosphere of the room.

"And how do you explain the fact that when Sunny phoned you at Sonja's to ask you for help with her summer school project, you weren't there?"

"Er, we went out, and—"

"And when I spoke to Sonja's mother, she said you hadn't made any plans to come for tea at all!" her mother continued the tirade before Maya had a chance to think on her feet.

"I didn't—"

"—bother to tell us the truth?" her father chipped in, with a thunderous look. "Like you didn't tell us about taking Ravi along on some outing with the photographic club you've joined

159

– just another little thing that seems to have slipped your mind?"

Brigid was right, then, Maya thought to herself in panic, aware that even Marcus seemed to be turning traitor, settled into her mother's lap and staring coolly at her. *Ravi couldn't manage to keep the secret to himself...*

"And where has this come from?" asked her mother, holding up a green plastic bag. It contained Joe's camera and a folder that included the old school photos she'd finally unearthed in the attic, her more recent efforts from the sleepover at Sonja's – as well as the picture from the album of her father and the mystery girl.

Maya suddenly realised that everything comes in threes and she was just about to get her third – and biggest – lecture of the day.

CHAPTER 19

• •

OTHER SECRETS AND PAST LIVES

"Who told you?" asked Maya, not able to believe that Brigid had betrayed her trust.

"Your sister. She overheard you talking to Brigid about this photography nonsense this afternoon," Nina Joshi replied, folding her arms across her chest.

"Sunny! How *dare* she—"

"How dare she nothing!" her dad bellowed. "We're very glad that at least one of our daughters is responsible! Do you realise how serious this is, going behind our backs? And as for Brigid, we'll have to speak to her too..."

Maya blinked hard and tried to contain her anger. She instantly remembered an article she'd read in one of her magazines that said it was vital to seem as much like a rational grown-up as possible in arguments with parents: start wailing or whining and you've lost it with them straight away.

"Look, it's not Brigid's fault, whatever Sunny's made out. I decided to join this club and I'm sorry I didn't tell you, but I didn't think you'd approve," said Maya as calmly as she could, which was difficult, faced with the contained fury of her parents.

"Approve? Of course we don't approve!" snapped her mother. "You've got sixth form coming up and some serious studying ahead. A-levels mean commitment. You spend quite enough of your free time as it is with your friends."

"Free time? You make it sound like I'm in prison – exercise privileges will be granted for good behaviour!" Maya snapped back before she could check herself.

"Don't be cheeky, Miss!" her father boomed. "You know exactly what we mean. We allow you plenty of freedom—"

"But you *don't*!" Maya protested. "I'm not like any of my friends; I can't just go to the cinema on the spur of the moment – I have to check that it's all right with you first. I can't just suddenly decide on a whim to wander round to Sonja's for a chat – I have to book it two weeks in advance!"

"You're being facetious!" her mother responded. "All we're trying to do is get the balance right between getting you to work hard and have time to yourself."

"Well, you *haven't* got the balance right!" said Maya, trying hard to rein in her runaway emotions.

"That's for us to decide!" her father bellowed.

"Dad – that's the point! It's *not* for you and Mum to decide, as if I haven't got a brain or an opinion of my own!"

"Don't be silly! You're still a child, and—"

"Look at me! I'm *not* a child! And even if I was, there should still be some decisions that are left down to me, like what hobbies I choose to have..."

"But when it's something that will ultimately affect your work at sixth form, which could in turn jeopardise your future career—"

"Dad, this is *why* I didn't tell you, because you make all these judgements about things without discussing them. I mean, of *course* you want to be involved in the major things in my life, but why can't it be something the three of us talk about together, rather than you two just laying down the law all the time?"

"You say that, but how can we trust your judgement if you go around lying about things like this?" her mother rebuked irritatingly, spreading out the photos from the plastic bag as if they were evidence in the case against Maya.

Feeling exhausted in the two-against-one battle of words, Maya was momentarily stumped. But as she drew breath, ready to push her point again, she heard her mother gasp.

"What's wrong?" asked Sanjay Joshi, rising to his feet and striding over quickly to his wife's side.

"It's– it's nothing. Just a surprise," she muttered, still staring down at the photos she'd randomly spread out in front of her.

Maya moved a couple of steps in from the doorway and tried to see what had caught her mother's attention so suddenly.

It was the dog-eared photo of her father and the mystery girl.

"I just haven't seen this for a long time. I didn't know we still had it..." her mother continued quietly.

Sanjay Joshi picked up the photo and stared at it.

"Where did you get this?" he asked Maya, the anger in his voice now gone.

"The attic – it was in an old album I found in a box," she answered, noticing that her father's hand was gently rubbing her mother's shoulder in a comforting manner. "Who is she?"

Maya felt her nerves jangling in anticipation of his reply. Judging from their reaction, the girl wasn't just another student or a family friend who could be casually explained away.

"She was the girl my parents wanted me to marry," her father said simply.

• • •

Sitting around the kitchen table, Maya poured everyone another cup of tea and felt strangely elated, despite the downcast expressions on her parents' faces.

"...and I was hardly the perfect prospective daughter-in-law, having a Muslim father and a white, Protestant mother," shrugged Nina Joshi as she added to her husband's explanation of the arranged marriage he'd spurned.

"My parents had seemed very liberal and caring up till that point," Maya's father elaborated. "But once I'd said no to the nice Hindu girl they'd chosen, and then told them about your mother, they made it very clear that it was the family... or her."

"So at the time you were introduced to this girl, you already knew that you loved Mum?" Maya asked her father, who'd rolled up his shirt sleeves and looked uncharacteristically ruffled, yet also more relaxed than she'd ever seen him.

"By that point," he answered her, looking directly into his wife's eyes, "we'd already been seeing each other in secret, for about..."

"...for about two years," Nina Joshi prompted him with a smile.

Secretly having a relationship? thought Maya. *And they worry about me doing some silly hobby behind their backs?*

"So is that why you're not really in touch with the rest of your family?" asked Maya, a whole chunk of her history now falling into place.

"Yes," her father nodded. "We had a strained relationship for a while then once my parents moved to Canada to be closer to your uncle, well..."

Maya was listening to a sad story of intolerance and estrangement – and she'd never been so happy. Her parents had never been so candid and open with her; sitting telling her about the unhappy circumstances of their fledgling relationship. They'd never treated her more like an adult.

There was, Maya realised joyously, no going back.

• • •

Ten minutes' walk away, at a small terraced house across from the park, Joe sat in front of the TV, randomly flicking through the channels with the remote control.

"Don't do that, Joe, love," said his mum, blinking uncomfortably at the rapidly flashing images.

"Sorry," Joe mumbled, stopping at some animal documentary and tossing the remote on to the sofa beside him.

Susie Gladwin blinked uncomfortably again as some unsuspecting antelope who'd been admiring the scenery was suddenly pounced on by a lioness.

"Do we have to watch this?" she asked squeamishly, closing one eye to lessen the impact of the unpleasant events unfolding on screen.

"Sorry!" he said sarcastically, picking the remote up and flicking over to some mind-numbing game show instead. Sometimes his mother seemed so naïve that Joe felt as if *he* was the parent and *she* was the kid. And that could be a real burden.

"Joe," said his mother after a few seconds' silence. "Is something wrong? You've been a bit, well, *funny* since you came back from your dad's..."

Joe ground his teeth and knew that this was the time he'd have to go for it – as Maya had said, he needed to get everything out in the open.

Here goes, he thought as he turned and

looked at his doe-eyed mum, her face full of maternal concern.

"Yeah, there's a couple of things actually," he began, dreading telling her the first bit in case she cried, and dreading confronting her with the second in case she cried again. "Mum, Gillian had a miscarriage when I was at Dad's."

"Oh, poor girl!" she gasped, clasping her hands together.

It wasn't the reaction Joe had expected. Why wasn't his mother more distressed at the idea of his father starting a new family?

"Do you understand, Mum?" he pressed her, in case she'd missed the point. "They were going to have a baby."

"Well, it was only a matter of time, wasn't it?" she answered him. "Gillian's a young woman; of course she'd want a child of her own with your father, instead of a hulking big stepson like you!"

She's making a joke, Joe realised, staring at his mother in amazement. *Why is she taking all this so well?*

"Well, there was something else, Mum," he went on, wondering how she'd react to the next thing he had to say.

"Yes, dear?" she smiled at him.

"When we were talking, Dad said... Dad said

that he wasn't the only one who'd been seeing someone else when the two of you were together."

"Oh, he told you that, did he?" Susie Gladwin nodded, a slight flush on her round cheeks. "And did he explain why I 'saw' someone else?"

"Uh, no," Joe replied, again surprised to see how calmly his mother was taking things; she was normally such as fusser and flusterer.

"Well," she said, folding her hands neatly on her lap as if she were about to tell him a bedtime story, "it was a good few months between your father telling me he'd met Gillian and him eventually deciding whether to leave us or give her up."

"I didn't know that!" Joe interrupted. "I thought it all happened really quickly!"

"Joe, you were barely thirteen – I wasn't going to burden you with all the gory details," she told him matter-of-factly. "Anyway, as you can imagine, that was a miserable time for me. And at that time, I met someone who listened and sympathised, and yes, it did go further once. I ended up telling your father and he got dreadfully upset, and that's when he finally decided to choose Gillian."

"But that wasn't fair – he didn't have any right

to be annoyed with you when he was still seeing her!" Joe blurted out.

"No, but love isn't fair, Joe. You might find that out one day," his mother said gently, while giving him a questioning look.

Joe had already learned this lesson. If love was fair, Kerry would be besotted with him instead of his best friend.

"But who was the man you saw and why didn't you tell me all of this before?"

"I didn't tell you because I didn't want to turn you against your dad; us breaking up had nothing to do with you," his mum shrugged. "And, despite the fact that you just see me as the sock-washer and meal-maker round here, I do have a private life. I don't really want to talk about something that happened a long time ago just now."

Joe felt a shock wave pass through him. It was as if he was seeing his mother in a whole new light; as if he had completely misunderstood her for the past four years. He'd always felt protective of her – the spurned, downtrodden little wife who'd been traumatised by her husband's desertion. And he'd felt resentful of his father too, not just for leaving them, but for landing the responsibility for looking after his mum unfairly but squarely on Joe's shoulders alone.

Now, staring at her, he realised that his mother was a lot stronger than he'd ever given her credit for. In fact, she had probably got over his father leaving far quicker than Joe had.

It struck him too that he didn't have to be his mother's protector any more. And, although he knew he'd never feel particularly close to his father, Joe saw that he didn't have to waste his energies hating his dad for his mother's sake any more.

The shock wave passed, and with it Joe felt a weight lift off his shoulders.

CHAPTER 20

● ●

AND THE WINNER IS...

"Nervous?"

Maya turned the source of the voice and found herself staring into a sheepish-looking face.

"I'm fine, Billy," she answered him, resisting the urge to point out that with more than a hundred entries to the Peacock Trust's competition, all of whom were probably a hundred times more experienced than her, Maya didn't see much point in being nervous. "And you?"

"Well, you know..." he smiled.

"What did you decide to enter in the end?" she asked, remembering he'd told her at their not-so-great date on Wednesday that he'd been stuck between a photo of a friend in mid-air heading a football and a shot he'd taken of a girl mid-conversation at the fair.

"I went for the girl," he nodded, slightly distracted by the kerfuffle of people stepping up to the dais close by them in the gallery's huge white entrance hall.

"Looks like this is it – good luck everyone!" said Alex, leaning over towards Maya, Ashleigh and Billy, before repeating the message to the rest of the photographic club members who were clustered around him.

Gazing back through the crowded hall, Maya focused in on Sonja and Matt and the others, all standing together at the back of the room. She laughed as she saw them all wave and make cartoon crossed-finger gestures at her.

As she turned back to face the front, Maya's eye was caught by a group of people pushing their way through the swing doors into the hall, and her heart beat with pride and excitement. They'd come: her parents, with Sunny *and* Brigid, and probably Ravi too, although he was too short to see above the throng.

Things had been better at home since the big bust-up on Wednesday and there was no mention again of Maya giving up the club. But she hadn't wanted to rock the boat by asking them to come to the gallery today.

So who told them? she wondered as the

gallery spokesperson began her introductory speech.

"...and a brilliant selection of portraits..." she heard as her mind raced between the amazing notion that her parents had made the effort to support her, and the awkwardness she felt realising that Billy was still standing at her side.

"...hard to make a selection from all this talent..."

What was he thinking?

Does he think he blew it with me on Wednesday? Or is he so thick-skinned he didn't twig that the headache was just an excuse to get away? she wondered, finding herself clapping as the third prize winner was announced.

Her eyes travelled from the newly revealed photo of a smiling old lady to the young teenage boy who went up to shake hands and accept his prize, without taking either of them in.

Sonja was right – I over-reacted, Maya thought, sneaking a sideways glance at Billy. *He may have been a bit clumsy in what he was saying, and he might not even be my type in the long run, but I didn't really give him much of a chance...*

Suddenly, she realised that Billy was staring at her with his pale blue eyes and a grin a mile wide. Her stomach did a backward somersault.

Did he just read my mind? she panicked, before hearing the words coming out of his mouth.

"Go on! Go up!" Billy laughed, pushing her gently on the back with his hand.

"What?" she asked him, dimly aware of a screech of cheering and whooping coming from somewhere at the back of the hall.

"You won second prize, Maya!"

She stared at him for a split second, before being propelled on to the stage by everyone in her club, and finding a shiny new camera case (heavy enough to know it contained a camera) in her hands.

"Well done!" said the woman from the gallery above the noise of clapping. Maya managed a cursory glance at the portrait she'd taken of her friends before she was back by Billy's side, shaking and stunned by the surprise and the unexpected flash of a bulb, courtesy of the local paper's photographer.

At least I'll be able to give Joe his dad's camera back, she managed to reason, her practical side showing through, despite how unsettled she felt.

"...and by sheer coincidence, the first prize..." Maya caught the woman saying as Alex congratulated her and a wave of gasps and clapping erupted all around.

"Woah! Yes!! Well done, Billy!" Alex erupted into a yell, his arm still around Maya.

She watched as Billy went forward and collected a camera and tripod as first prize winner. There were more flashes as the local paper went to work again, illuminating Billy and the portrait he had taken.

Of me... Maya spotted, her heart lurching in shock.

It was Maya all right – looking bewildered but beautiful in profile as she contemplated two old men, who were staring back at her open-mouthed, as if they were beholding the rarest, most exotic lotus blossom.

"Maya!" shouted Billy, motioning her to join him. Once again, Maya felt her fellow club mates propel her on to the stage.

"That's me," she found herself saying stupidly to him. "At the fair, trying to talk to those farmers."

"Yep," grinned Billy as the paper's photographer yelled for them both to look towards him.

Maya felt Billy's lips on her cheek as the white light of the flash blinded her again.

• • •

"Well, Brigid told us that her niece was entering a photo of Ravi playing with piglets, so we had to come," said her father, smiling warmly at his daughter. "We'll have to find him – I think all your other school friends took him off to look for it."

Sonja – who'd stayed behind with Maya as she stood by her winning entry, being congratulated by and shaking the hands of people she didn't know – gave her an unseen isn't-this-brilliant? squeeze around the waist.

"But, of course, we're very proud of you too, for getting second prize," added her mother as people milled around the gallery, at last having the chance to look at all the entries dotted around the walls. "Aren't we, Sunny?"

"Yes, Mummy!" Sunita purred sweetly at her mother, before giving her sister an insincere smile.

"Thanks, Mum," said Maya, pleased, but also aware that the winning part had a lot to do with her parents' new-found approval of her hobby. And that Sunny's appearance today had more to do with curiosity than any desire to show Maya her support.

Still, she thought to herself, *who's complaining?*

"And what about that portrait of Maya winning, Mrs Joshi?" asked Sonja, keen to milk her friend's success for all it was worth in front of her parents.

"Yes – in fact we're just off to have a closer look at it, aren't we, Sanjay?" Nina Joshi said to her husband, looking over at the stand which held the winning entry. Hovering beside it, surrounded by friends and family, was Billy, who gave Maya a shy smile and a wave.

"What's going on there?" Maya heard Sonja hiss.

"I don't know – it's too early to say," Maya hissed back, thinking she was referring to Billy. Instead, she found Sonja staring intently at Maya's black and white photo.

"It's all looking suspiciously lovey-dovey in this – well, apart from yours truly, I'm sad to say. And Joey, of course."

"What are you on about?" asked Maya, leaning in towards the photo.

"From that loved-up look on her face, Kerry is obviously waving at her knight in shining apron, who's out of shot somewhere," Sonja pointed. "But here's something more interesting – notice the way Catrina and Matt are staring all gooey-eyed at each other? It's not starting all over again, is it?"

Maya had to admit, on closer inspection, that the sidelong look her two friends were giving each other did seem full of longing.

But that look wasn't what concerned Maya most: now that she was taking a second look, she realised that Joe wasn't paying attention to Sonja at all, as she'd assumed when she'd first printed the picture. He seemed to be staring past her, with the soulful, sad look of unrequited love at... Kerry.

Well, they do say the camera never lies, thought Maya, aware that she'd stumbled on one of Joe's deep, dark secrets. And it wasn't just the fact that she knew he hated being called 'Joey'...

Sugar
SECRETS...

...& Lust

SNEAK PREVIEW!

Sonja had decided a while ago that it was about time she had a boyfriend. She hadn't had any serious love interest for months. Most people who knew Sonja considered her to be a ten out of ten on the babe-o-meter. *Easily*. She had long blonde hair, penetrating blue eyes, perfect bone structure, a figure to die for and great dress sense. She literally turned heads in the street.

When she thought about it, Sonja realised that she probably *was* too fussy. But rightly so. She had no intention of going out with just anyone. Most of the guys who came into contact with her and who fancied their chances were given the knock back. Politely, of course.

But Sonja was no wilting wallflower either. If she saw someone she fancied, she had no qualms about going straight over and chatting them up. Not in a full-on way like Catrina, but *subtly*, sussing out whether they had a brain behind the good looks. She was quite measured in her approach to guys – they had to be good-looking, but if there wasn't a spark in the conversation as well, forget it. She didn't have the time to waste on pretty – but vacant – faces.

The dilemma with Kyle was that they'd never actually *met*. Somehow she was going to have to find a way to chat him up in the shop or in the street. Even super-assured Sonja found that prospect daunting. Hence the need for a plan, which she was now ready to put into action.

Pulling her bright red paddle brush through her hair, Sonja glanced at herself in the full-length mirror in the hallway and gave herself a quick once-over. Straight-cut pants, strappy low-heeled sandals, a bright blue T-shirt, lightly bronzed skin and no make-up other than a touch of lip gloss was as much effort as Sonja felt she needed to make. It was as much effort as she *ever* made, not being into the caked-on make-up look (hence the disagreement with Cat on Saturday night) nor the tarty clothes scene.

"You'll do," she muttered to herself as she grabbed her bag from the sideboard and headed for the front door.

The stroll through town to the centre of Winstead on such a fabulously hot day was uplifting. She almost forgot her reason for going as she breathed in the heat and listened to the gentle breeze rustling the trees. Being a Sunday, the roads were quieter than normal, and what traffic did pass by seemed to be moving at a much slower pace, in keeping with the laid-back feel of the day.

When Sonja got to the Plaza, Winstead's shopping centre, she went inside and wandered towards the new sports shop, looking in casually as she passed. Unable to see Kyle, she sauntered on to the little café at the centre of the mall and ordered a coffee. Then she sat down and spent the next twenty minutes watching the world go by.

Just as she decided it was time to head back and go right into the shop this time, Sonja saw Kyle wander right past her. Wow! He looked tastier than ever. And, even better, he seemed to be on his own. Perfect! Time to put her plan into action.

Before he was able to get too far away from her, Sonja leapt up from her seat and chased after him.

"Ben! Ben! Wait up!" she called as she sped towards his rapidly disappearing (and very cute) rear.

Not surprisingly, he didn't turn round. Directly behind him now, Sonja reached up and tapped him on the shoulder.

"Ben?" she said again. He stopped and turned to her, a confused look on his face.

"Oh! I'm sorry!" said Sonja, smiling sweetly, then looking at the ground in a show of embarrassment. Returning her gaze to his, she added, "I thought you were someone else."

Kyle looked moderately taken aback but pleased at the same time as he took in the vision standing in front of him.

"Sorry to disappoint you," he grinned, blushing. "I could change my name if that's any help..."

Sonja smiled back and thought *so far so good*. "That's okay – and it's not a disappointment."

Anyone else would have cringed at such a line, but not Sonja. She was confident enough to carry it off and make it sound like the most sincere thing she had ever said. And Kyle certainly seemed to appreciate it: His grin just got broader, his face got redder with embarrassment and his eyes popped even further out of his head as he so obviously thought *Wow, what a babe!*

"So, uh... were you supposed to be meeting this Ben here, then?" he asked, trying to keep the conversation going.

"Ooh, no, I came into town *on my own*," answered Sonja pointedly. "Ben's the boyfriend of a friend of mine and you just looked like him from the back."

"Oh, right." They stopped talking and looked at each other for a moment, then Kyle picked up the conversation again. "Uh, it's my lunchbreak... I was actually just heading off for a coffee. D'you fancy one?"

"Mmm, that'd be great," replied Sonja, thinking *Yeesss, I'm in here!*

COULD YOU MAKE THE FIRST MOVE?

● ●

Looks like Sonja's about to get the lad of her choice, but what about you? You might like a boy, but doing something about it takes guts. Have you got what it takes?

(1) When it comes to getting to know each other, do you leave it to the lad to make the first move?

a) Yes, I'd be *far* too embarrassed to approach him!

b) Not necessarily – but I don't know if I could do it, to be honest.

c) 'Course not! It's only fair to take a turn.

(2) Have you ever chatted someone up?

a) Me? No way!

b) Me? No, but I've wanted to!

c) Yes! Haven't you?

(3) For you, making the first move would mean...

a) Looking in his direction, then looking shyly away.

b) Looking in his direction, then smiling.

c) Looking in his direction, then finding an excuse to get on over there, pronto.

(4) You hear from a friend of a friend that a boy really likes you. That gives you...

a) Hope that something might happen between the two of you.

b) The confidence to talk to him.

c) An excuse to start some full-on flirting.

(5) You've seen a lad you like, but he's given you no indication that he likes you back. You think:

a) Oh well, that's that, then.

b) He might notice me at some point, you never know.

c) I'll try chatting him up anyway. Nothing ventured, nothing gained!

(6) What would your girl mates think if you made the first move?

a) They'd be amazed.

b) They'd be impressed.

c) They're used to it – they know that's my style!

(7) What do you think lads make of girls who take the initiative?

a) They'd think they were coming on too strong.

b) They'd probably be flattered and flustered at the same time.

c) They're well chuffed, in my experience!

8 You've heard that someone's a bit of a bad lad. Would you that put you off making a move?

a) Definitely.

b) Yes; at least, I'd wait and find out a lot more about him.

c) No. I've got to find things out for myself haven't I?

9 If you got knocked back, how would that make you feel?

a) Devastated – that's why I never make the first move!

b) Pretty lousy, but at least I'd know I tried.

c) A bit put out – but you can't win 'em all.

10 You think being subtle when you fancy someone is...

a) The only way I could operate when it comes to lads.

b) A nice way of letting someone know you like them, without making a fool of yourself.

c) A waste of time – life's too short!

NOW CHECK OUT HOW YOU SCORED...

SCORES

• •

Mostly a

You're shy and unsure when it comes to boys, and that could mean you're in danger of letting chances slip through your fingers. Your approach is so subtle that the lads you like probably think you have zero interest, so never bother trying to get to know you better! Maybe you could take a leaf out of Sonja's book and try to be a little more encouraging. OK, so you don't have the confidence to make the first move, but you should at least let *him* know that you'd be happy if *he* did!

Mostly b

It takes a lot of courage to make the first move, but you think you might be up for it if the right person came along. And that's the key: if you take your time and make sure that the lad you like is right for you (and you're pretty sure he likes you back) then it's definitely worth being bold. After all, he might be as nervous as you, and someone's got to take a step towards making something happen!

Mostly c

You're practically fearless when it comes to letting someone know you like them. In loads of ways that's great; it shows that you're confident and happy with yourself, and you're not afraid of taking chances and getting a "no" for an answer! On the other hand, it means that you can sometimes land yourself in trouble, by leaping into situations without stopping to think first! Take care – you might discover that your heart is a lot more fragile than you think...

Sugar

SECRETS...

...& Lust

DATE-DEPRIVATION!
Sonja laments the lack of fanciable
blokes around, then two come along at
once.

MYSTERY STRANGER!
One is seriously cute, but why is he
looking for Anna?

LUST!
Will Sonja choose Kyle or Owen –
or both?!

*Some secrets are just too good to
keep to yourself!*

Collins
An Imprint of HarperCollinsPublishers
www.fireandwater.com

Order Form

To order direct from the publishers, just make a list of the titles you want and fill in the form below:

Name ....

Address ....

....

....

Send to: Dept 6, HarperCollins Publishers Ltd, Westerhill Road, Bishopbriggs, Glasgow G64 2QT.

Please enclose a cheque or postal order to the value of the cover price, plus:

UK & BFPO: Add £1.00 for the first book, and 25p per copy for each additional book ordered.

Overseas and Eire: Add £2.95 service charge. Books will be sent by surface mail but quotes for airmail despatch will be given on request.

A 24-hour telephone ordering service is available to Visa and Access card holders: 0141- 772 2281

Collins
An *Imprint* of HarperCollins*Publishers*